NEXT

Negative Evaluation and Xchange Trade

Table of Contents

CHAPTER ONE

The low hum filled the room like the droning of an ancient machine left running far too long—steady, faintly irritating, and the only sound interrupting the stillness beneath the harsh, fluorescent lights. The people seated in neat, regimented rows appeared almost embalmed in their uniforms of power suits, their gazes glazed over as they sipped on coffee with grim determination. This wasn't the sort of silence that spoke of charged anticipation. Instead, it carried the unmistakable weight of apathy and obligatory attendance, held together by caffeine fumes and the reliable monotony of government salaries. At the front of the room, Dr. Meredith Grayson took her place with an air that demanded both attention and restraint. She was the head sociologist—a title that, among those familiar with her, was often paired with her reputation for casting looks of disdain at students daring enough to approach her at department mixers. Tonight, though, she wasn't exuding 'high-minded academic' as much as 'calculating mastermind on the brink of unveiling her diabolical brainchild.' The kind of presence that teetered between genius and menace.

Her fingers hovered momentarily over the remote in her hand, then clicked with a firm precision that revealed a bold, attention-grabbing title on the screen behind her:

NEXT: *A Revolutionary Approach to Relationship Management.*

She adjusted her glasses, a practiced motion that lent her a certain sharpness, as if she could slice through the room's haze of indifference with a single glance. When she spoke, her voice was cool, clinical, stripped of any sentimentality that might soften her message. "Marriages, as we know, are crumbling," she said, her tone deliberately measured. "Roughly half of them end in divorce, and for many that persist, well—let's just say the arrangement more closely resembles a cold war ceasefire than any romantic ideal."

Her words struck a discordant note, rousing a reaction from the otherwise immobile crowd. From the far end of the room, an elderly senator shifted uncomfortably, his face wrinkling in a practiced expression of skepticism. "So?" he challenged, his voice a dry scoff. "Isn't that just the way things are?"

Dr. Grayson's eyes flashed with a brief, almost imperceptible flicker of irritation. "No, Senator, it isn't," she replied, her voice steely. She didn't pause for him to interject further. "The disintegration of the family unit is fueling a range of systemic issues that extend far beyond personal disappointment," she continued, her gaze sweeping over the room. "We're talking about tangible, measurable fallout—

lost work productivity, declining birth rates, skyrocketing therapy costs. And," she added with a pointedly disdainful glance, "a seemingly endless market for self-help books that promise personal transformation but seldom deliver."

With a calculated flick of her wrist, Dr. Grayson clicked the remote once more. The screen blipped, then faded into the sharp, sterile glow of an interface that looked equal parts sleek and sinister. The logo appeared next, coldly modern, its minimalist design giving off an unsettling air of impersonal efficiency. It read:

NEXT: *Negative Evaluation and Xchange Trade*

The words glinted in a shade of steel-blue, the kind of color more suited to the branding of a law enforcement database than anything meant to deal with personal relationships. It had the clinical, slightly intimidating feel of an app built to erase attachments with all the ease of hitting "delete" on an email marked as spam.

"This," Dr. Grayson resumed with a subtle, almost imperceptible smirk, "is our solution. NEXT offers a streamlined way for users to publicly list their partners. Think of it as a social media profile, but instead of highlighting accomplishments and happy memories, it zeroes in on everything you despise about your spouse." She paused, letting the gravity of her words sink in, her eyes glinting with the thrill of unveiling something simultaneously abhorrent and revolutionary. "We call these 'evaluations.' They're posted publicly, so anyone can see them. And any interested party who thinks they could do better—or simply finds the trade appealing—can submit an offer."

The audience collectively recoiled, a series of grimaces spreading across the faces of senators, agency heads, and departmental staffers alike. Dr. Grayson's smile only broadened, watching as her words turned in their minds like a cold knife. "It's a, shall we say, more efficient approach to managing relationships."

The silence that followed was thick, bordering on palpable, stretching out as the audience wrestled with the implications. These were people accustomed to endorsing innovative, even unorthodox policies in the name of so-called progress. But this? This was something else entirely—a modern-day marketplace for marital grievances, wrapped up in slick UX design and a tagline that barely concealed its inherent cruelty.

A figure finally shifted at the front row. It was the Chief of Operations, Jurgens, a man who'd spent two decades pushing forward initiatives he seldom fully understood. He adjusted his glasses and leaned forward, his expression caught somewhere between bafflement and intrigue.

"So... if I understand correctly, this is essentially a 'worst of' list for relationships? That's what we're giving people?"

Dr. Grayson met his gaze with a calm, unblinking stare, nodding as if the simplicity of his summary delighted her. "Precisely, Jurgens. We're just reflecting the unvarnished truth. And in doing so, we're helping couples cut through years of unnecessary arguments and exorbitant legal fees." Her voice remained poised, but there was a subtle edge of satisfaction, as though she'd just unveiled the future of relationship management in a single, ruthless stroke.

Dr. Grayson swept a hand toward the screen, indicating the stark interface and the disarmingly simple setup of the platform. Its minimalist design radiated a kind of dystopian charm—clean, utilitarian, almost soothing in its ruthlessness. "It's fast, it's transparent," she continued. "We move people in and out of relationships with efficiency, all based on honest, user-generated feedback. No sugarcoating, no misleading profiles, no 'perfect match' nonsense. No one's left with decades of regret."

At the opposite end of the table, a hesitant hand rose, followed by the uncertain voice of a well-known tech mogul. He was accustomed to innovative but comparatively benign products, not initiatives that brushed up against ethical dilemmas with such bold disregard. "But Dr. Grayson," he murmured, his voice shaky with caution, "isn't there a risk here? We're essentially treating people as... inventory. Won't there be psychological repercussions?"

Dr. Grayson rolled her eyes with barely concealed impatience, her dismissive wave seeming to scatter the concerns as if they were trivial inconveniences. "Psychological repercussions?" she repeated, her tone bordering on mocking. "As if divorce doesn't leave scars? We're improving lives here, not complicating them. With NEXT, we reduce the drawn-out emotional suffering, we offer a quick solution, and in time, this will stabilize family structures—eventually." She leaned forward, her eyes glinting with a fervor reserved for visionaries or mad scientists. "And consider the data! We'll have metrics on compatibility, comprehensive data on what works and what fails in relationships, all at a scale that no other institution has dared attempt. This is revolutionary, people."

The board members exchanged uneasy glances, the kind that seemed to recognize the potential for catastrophe but couldn't quite look away. Meanwhile, the faint smell of scorched coffee permeated the air, mingling with an intangible sense of regret. One of the finance officers cleared his throat, his fingers wrapped tensely around his cup.

Dr. Grayson pressed on, her enthusiasm growing, voice adopting a near-religious zeal.

"Just imagine it," she continued, her tone softened to something almost reverent. "No more awkward holiday dinners with resentful spouses, no more restless nights spent agonizing over settling. With NEXT, everyone gets exactly what they signed up for, and when they don't? Boom." She snapped her fingers for emphasis. "NEXT takes care of the rest. Quick, painless, effective."

The Chief of Operations, Jurgens, leaned back, his hand stroking his chin as he stared at the screen, a glint of contemplation in his narrowed eyes. "Well," he said finally, in a slow, measured tone, "it's... innovative. But perhaps we should consider the potential for unforeseen effects? This is uncharted territory."

Dr. Grayson's thin smile was so practiced it felt like part of her professional uniform. "Unforeseen?" she echoed, an edge of mockery slipping into her tone. "We've accounted for every variable that matters." She paused, then shrugged slightly. "Well, most of them, at least. We'll call any hiccups 'growing pains.' And besides," she added, her smirk turning sly, "everyone knows marriage is already something of a nightmare."

Her words lingered, hanging in the stale air as the board members looked at one another, their hesitant nods suggesting a horrifying realization. Perhaps, as horrifying as it sounded, this was the future. It was logical. Efficient. A bit monstrous, but what real progress didn't demand a few sacrifices? The vote was called. Only one hand didn't rise in approval. And with that lone abstention, NEXT was approved, the cold wheels of progress set in motion.

As they left the room, the unease followed them. A few officials murmured, already predicting the chaos that might follow. But others looked curiously excited, eager to see the populace embrace this digital "solution."

Dr. Grayson paused at the door, listening to the faint murmur from the boardroom. She allowed a satisfied smile to slip. NEXT was only the beginning, after all.

Valerie Porter's mornings unfolded like an unrelenting race, each second slipping through her fingers as she scrambled to meet the demands of the day. By the time the sun crept high enough to filter through the kitchen window, spilling pale light onto the countertops, Valerie was already well behind. The sharp scent of burnt toast clung to the air, mingling with the chaotic clatter of mismatched Tupperware lids, her hands moving on autopilot as she slapped together another hasty breakfast for her five children. Each one's name was an echo—a reminder—of a different man, some still present in her life, others long gone, their faces fading into the past. None of them shared the same father. Her mind wandered briefly to the children's origins, but she quickly pushed it away. She couldn't afford to dwell on the fact that each child symbolized yet another failed attempt to create something resembling a stable family. One of them, an energetic boy diagnosed with high-functioning ADHD, demanded her attention every couple of minutes, his endless stream of questions and impulses creating an exhausting rhythm to the morning. Another, a sweet-faced troublemaker with a wild streak, was always on the move, running from one school administration office to the next, with his growing list of expulsions and behavior reports to prove it. Her youngest, a girl who had just begun to form sentences but had yet to master the art of keeping her hands out of trouble, was particularly adept at spilling cereal onto the floor just as Valerie thought she might have a brief moment of peace to herself. The others were a mix of ages, each one a patchwork of quirks, tantrums, and unspoken needs that Valerie had learned to navigate, but only just.

And yet, no matter how hard she tried, none of them were David's kids.

David was something different entirely. He wasn't just another name from her past, another fleeting connection or mistake. He was a possibility, the one person who could have—who still could—become the rock she never had. But in the midst of the mess of her mornings, of the clanging dishes and the constant pull of her children's demands, David was an ideal that felt both distant and elusive, something too far out of reach to focus on for too long. Valerie paused for a moment, looking at the faces of her kids—her five beautiful, exhausting kids—and then glanced at the clock. There was no time for these thoughts now. There never was.

David. Her current husband, the man who had been with her through every high and low, but who might as well have been a roommate at this point. Their marriage, once a hopeful partnership, had long ago slipped into the abyss of routine, and now, it was more about surviving the days together than actually living them. Valerie couldn't remember the last time David had kissed her in a way that didn't feel like an obligation—like something they were both required to do, part of some awkward, unspoken social contract they'd entered into but had long since forgotten the details of. The intimacy had drained away so slowly, so imperceptibly, that she hadn't noticed until one day she woke up to find it gone. In its place was an emptiness that neither of them dared acknowledge.

Their relationship had become so devoid of passion, so utterly mechanical, that it was easier to pretend they were both content than to face the harsh truth—that they were more strangers than spouses.

"Mom, where's my—?"

Valerie barely registered the voice, distracted by the familiar chaos that surrounded her. She looked up just in time to see Jason, her teenage son, leaning against the kitchen table with his arms crossed. His posture screamed frustration, his teenage defiance filling the room like an unmistakable storm cloud. Jason was the one who looked most like his biological father, the man she'd left in a haze of drunken decision-making, only to realize later that he had been just as emotionally unavailable as David had become. Jason's sharp edges—his anger, his mood swings, his unwillingness to trust anyone—were all traits she had seen before in his father, and they stung more than she cared to admit. Jason's tone was thick with teenage frustration, the kind that had become a constant fixture in their home, but Valerie only half-heard him as she fumbled to collect the last of her belongings, pulling her purse over her shoulder in a rush to get out the door. Another day of scraping by, of surviving, not living.

"Your shoes are by the door. Don't forget your lunch," she muttered, her voice as tired as the motions she was going through. The words fell flat in the chaos of the morning—unheard, unimportant, lost in the ever-growing list of things to do, things to manage, things that didn't matter enough for anyone to care. She didn't wait for Jason to respond, not that he ever did. She grabbed her keys, trying to block out the rising tension between them, the silence that had settled over her relationship with David, the ache in her chest that she couldn't name. She just needed to get through the day. That was all. She could worry about the rest later—if there was ever a later. Jason rolled his eyes but didn't offer a word of protest. The silence between them was thick, weighed down by everything that had gone unspoken—the resentment that had silently festered between them over the years, the quiet disappointment that hung in the air like an uninvited guest. It was as if there were an invisible wall now, one that had gradually grown taller and sturdier with each passing argument, each neglected conversation. Valerie had stopped trying to explain herself to him years ago. Who was she to teach him about responsibility, about relationships, when her own life was a patchwork of half-finished attempts, a constant mess she could hardly control? What right did she have to offer any advice when she couldn't even fix her own shattered pieces?

She grabbed her purse, the leather strap digging into her fingers as she yanked it from the counter. Her hand shook slightly, betraying the fatigue that had settled into her bones. Inside, she shoved receipts, a crumpled pack of gum, and an old bottle of aspirin into the cluttered abyss of her bag, each item as disconnected as the parts of her life. She had stopped seeing her therapist months ago, too worn down by the suffocating pressure of daily life to carve out a single hour a week to sit and untangle the wreckage of her mind. The thought of the therapist's office—of talking through the never-ending noise in her head—felt like a luxury she couldn't afford. Her bipolar disorder, the beast that lurked in the recesses of her psyche, was something she'd always struggled to manage. A storm that could shift from one extreme to the next in an instant, sweeping everything in its path. Some days, she was fine—functional, present, even normal. But other days, the storm was too much, too loud, too consuming. And when it got too overwhelming, the alcohol became the easiest escape. A few drinks, a quick buzz, and for a moment, the chaos inside her brain quieted, giving her just enough peace to breathe before the madness returned. It was a temporary fix, a band-aid that never quite stayed in place.

As she walked out the door, the sharp clack of her shoes echoed against the cracked pavement, each step a reminder that she was still moving forward—even if it felt like she was moving in circles. It was then, just as she was about to slip into the familiar solitude of her car, that she heard it.

"Valerie?"

The voice was a faint call, distant at first, as though it had been buried beneath the layers of her thoughts. She stopped mid-step, turning her head toward the sound, and there, standing on the sidewalk, was Tara. Valerie blinked, momentarily stunned. Tara, a friend she hadn't seen in months, was waving from the street, her smile as warm and familiar as the sun that had just begun to rise higher in the sky.

Valerie hesitated. For a moment, she wasn't sure if she was glad to see her or if the appearance of someone from her past was just another complication she wasn't ready to face.

"Val! Hey, girl, you hear about that new app—NEXT?"

Valerie stopped in her tracks, her curiosity piqued. "NEXT?" she asked, the word tumbling around in her mind, unfamiliar yet oddly intriguing. Tara's expression was a blend of mischief and amusement, and her voice held a note of excitement Valerie hadn't heard in a long time.

"Yeah," Tara said, leaning in with a conspiratorial smile, "it's this thing where you can trade your partner, like... like a damn marketplace. People post all the reasons their spouse drives them insane, every little thing that irritates them, and then, bam—someone else can swipe left or right, just like a dating app. It's insane, right? But apparently, it's taking off. People are already signing up, posting, browsing. It's, like, a whole movement."

Valerie felt a strange jolt, as if a long-buried nerve had been hit. The idea of "trading" David, of stepping out of the life she felt chained to, didn't seem as outrageous as it should have. For years, she'd told herself that she was just tired, that life was hard for everyone, that David was, in some obscure way, the best she could hope for. But what if she'd been wrong? What if she'd simply settled into something that had drained her of herself? Maybe, just maybe, there was someone out there who wouldn't look right through her. Someone who didn't find her messes exhausting or her chaos a burden. Someone who, God forbid, actually liked her disarray.

She smiled tightly at Tara, but her mind was racing. "Sounds like a mess."

Tara laughed, brushing off Valerie's hesitation. "Oh, it totally is. I mean, I'm not saying it's for everyone, but—" She shrugged. "I've been thinking about putting Mike on there. He's been unbearable lately. And who knows? Maybe I could find someone with a little more… patience, if you know what I mean."

Valerie nodded, her hand gripping her purse as she processed Tara's words. She offered her friend a faint wave before heading toward her car. As she drove away, the idea gnawed at her, sticking in her mind like a splinter. What would it be like to let go of David, even just to entertain the idea of trading him for a man who saw her, truly saw her? The thought of it left her torn—resentment mixing with something she hadn't felt in a long time. Hope. A tiny, dangerous spark of hope.

The house was quiet that night, steeped in the kind of silence that reminded her of everything she'd chosen to ignore. When she finally climbed into bed beside David, the mattress barely shifting as she lay down, she stared at the ceiling, her mind buzzing. She turned to her phone, and with a deep breath, searched for the NEXT app. The logo popped up on her screen, sleek and modern, with a tagline that read: *Redefine Relationships, One Evaluation at a Time.*

Her thumb hovered over the "Download" button. A part of her knew she shouldn't, that this app was likely another futile attempt at happiness, just another detour away from confronting the real issues between her and David. But another part of her—an angry, weary part that she'd silenced too many times—whispered, *Why not?* After all, what did she have to lose?

She downloaded the app, biting her lip as she set up her profile and scrolled through the "Post Partner" page. Her finger hovered over the "Post Partner" button, her heart pounding with anticipation and guilt. Would it really be that simple? Could she just put David up for trade and let fate handle the rest?

She glanced at David, asleep beside her, his breathing heavy, oblivious to her restlessness. In that moment, as she stared at her screen, she felt like she was standing on the edge of something unknown, a strange new world of possibility. What kind of man might she end up with? Would he be more patient, more attentive—or just another disappointment in a different form?

The idea was tempting, more tempting than she cared to admit. Her thumb hovered, trembling with the pull of a different life, a different future. And in the silence of their bedroom, she wondered if she'd finally found her way out.

CHAPTER TWO

David sat alone at the worn kitchen table, his gaze fixed on the crack in the wall that he'd been meaning to fix for months. The crack had grown wider over the years, creeping like an inevitable truth—one he kept ignoring in the hope it would somehow disappear on its own. He could still hear the kids settling down, the sounds of small, tired voices growing softer, and finally, fading into sleep. Now, all that remained was silence. The dull hum of the refrigerator was the only sound punctuating the stale air of a home he barely recognized as his own. He wasn't oblivious to Valerie's resentment; if anything, he felt it settle between them like a fog neither wanted to confront. They had once been a real team, at least he thought they had. They'd shared laughter, inside jokes, even quiet nights where words weren't needed. But somewhere along the way, that connection had unraveled. Conversations that once had been easy and open had shrunk into nothing more than obligatory exchanges about grocery lists, the kid's missing schoolwork, and the next round of late bills. What had once felt like a marriage, however imperfect, had transformed into a relentless march through days that looked exactly alike, as if they were both trapped in an endless loop. She had her world of frustration and silent disappointment, and he was left on an island, watching her drift away one inch at a time. The truth was, he wasn't even sure why he stayed. Yes, the kids anchored him—they were part of his life now, each bringing their own spark, their own need, and their own little messes. He loved them, even if he wasn't their biological father, and he knew they looked up to him, whether they'd admit it or not. And maybe that was part of the reason. He couldn't bear the thought of leaving them, of adding another layer of disappointment and instability to lives already complicated by so many moving parts. Walking away felt like shattering whatever fragile family they had left, and every time he thought about it, he stopped himself.

Deep down, he knew Valerie's anger had become something that couldn't just be "waited out." She blamed him for the lackluster life they now led, for the fact that they were just two tired people trying to hold everything together with too little to give and even less left for each other. And maybe, he thought, she wasn't wrong. The message hit David like a punch to the gut. He read it once, twice, then again, hoping he'd somehow misunderstood. But the words stayed the same, each one digging a little deeper. Valerie was actually considering listing him on NEXT—the app everyone was talking about, where people could turn their relationships into public yard sales, trading their partners like a used car or an old phone. The system was designed for efficiency, sure, but the thought of being reduced to a collection of complaints for strangers to swipe through made his skin crawl.

Sitting there in the dim kitchen, he felt the slow burn of anger stirring beneath his shock, but it was tangled with something else, something much harder to swallow. The sadness gnawed at him, a raw realization that this was where they'd ended up. Not with the honesty he'd once hoped they'd manage to salvage, not even with the messy finality of a fight that could lay everything bare, but with a digital profile, a summary of his faults she felt the world needed to see. All those tiny disappointments, the ways he'd failed to be the partner she'd needed or wanted, would be exposed in a format designed to be judged, commented on, even laughed at.

David clenched his jaw, staring down at the phone. So this was it? After years of shared memories and quiet struggles, after raising kids together and weathering the storms of life side by side, it was all coming down to a few lines on a screen? The humiliation simmered inside him, mixing with an ache he hadn't known he could still feel. For years, he'd told himself they'd just grown apart, that maybe this was the natural course of things. But the idea that she could turn him into a profile for strangers to critique and dismiss felt like a betrayal he hadn't been prepared for.

And then a darker question crept into his mind: was this really all he was to her now? Just a collection of grievances, a list of flaws, something to be traded off to the next willing participant?

David stared at the screen, his thumb hovering over the download button. He felt the bitterness seeping into him, threatening to drown out whatever fragments of love or respect remained. The idea of listing her first, of preemptively putting her faults on display, was both laughable and strangely appealing. After all, hadn't he put up with just as much? He could write pages on the emotional minefield he navigated daily, the coldness, the silent resentment that had replaced any trace of affection between them. For a second, the thought of flipping the script felt almost satisfying. But as his thumb lingered, he felt a sick churn in his stomach. Was this really who he wanted to be? Someone who retaliated by dragging their own wife through the mud? The longer he sat there, the more he recognized how far they'd fallen, both clawing for the moral low ground in a desperate attempt to make their pain known. His grip tightened on the phone as he forced himself to take a steady breath. Listing her on NEXT wouldn't solve anything; it would only confirm what they both feared—that they'd become so entangled in blame and bitterness, they couldn't find a way back to decency. And yet, the humiliation lingered. His own insecurities had always been easy to keep at bay—quiet fears of inadequacy, of not being enough for his family. But now, faced with the idea that she'd been cataloging his flaws, preparing to put them on public display, every doubt surged to the surface. Did she really believe he'd failed her on every count? Was there nothing left in their years together that she felt was worth keeping? The questions twisted inside him, leaving him feeling stripped bare, as if she'd already posted him on that virtual chopping block for all to see.

David placed the phone face-down on the table, letting the silence settle back around him. This wasn't just about pride; it was about dignity. He knew if he went down the same path as Valerie, there'd be nothing left of who he wanted to be. Maybe they were both teetering on the edge, but he wasn't ready to give in to that kind of ugliness, not yet.

As he scrolled through the app, he felt a pang of guilt. He was trying to get back at her, to make her feel the sting of rejection first. But his pride and frustration had clouded his judgment, and now he found himself staring at the blank profile screen, wondering if he could go through with it. Could he really reduce Valerie to a list of grievances, the way he feared she would do to him?

Just as he was about to close the app, he heard her footsteps from the hallway. He quickly stuffed his phone into his pocket and looked up to see her standing in the doorway, her face lit by the soft glow of her own phone screen. She didn't notice him at first, her attention focused entirely on the device in her hand. Her fingers moved quickly, typing with a cold precision that sent a chill through him.

He watched her for a moment, feeling the weight of betrayal settle heavy in his chest. She was so absorbed, so focused, that she hadn't even noticed him standing there. It was like he had disappeared, already reduced to nothing more than the grievances she was documenting. The years they'd spent together—every shared laugh, every argument, every hard-fought compromise—had led to this quiet, brutal moment. She was writing him out of her life, one petty line at a time.

David swallowed, his throat tight. Part of him wanted to grab the phone from her hand, confront her right then and there. He could demand to know how she saw him now, why she'd chosen to make him into a caricature of his worst traits, but he stayed rooted in place. Anger and sorrow warred within him, yet all he could feel was a kind of hollow acceptance. It was like watching a slow-motion train wreck he could do nothing to stop.

As she finished typing, she finally looked up, startled to find him watching her. She froze, her expression unreadable as she realized he had seen everything. For a split second, he thought he saw a flicker of guilt in her eyes, a flash of something vulnerable that quickly hardened into a guarded stare. She slipped the phone into her pocket, her fingers brushing against it as though it were some talisman of control she wasn't ready to let go of.

They stood in silence, the air between them thick with everything they couldn't bring themselves to say. He searched her face, hoping to find some hint of remorse, a sign that this was just a momentary lapse of judgment. But Valerie's gaze was steady, almost defiant, as if daring him to call her out on what she'd done.

"So," he finally managed, his voice rough. "This is where we're at now? Reducing each other to a few lines on a screen?"

She said nothing, her jaw tightening as her hand lingered near her pocket. She didn't deny it, didn't try to justify or explain. In that moment, he realized how far apart they truly were—two people who'd shared a life, a home, a family, yet had become strangers standing on opposite sides of a widening chasm.

"David..." she started, but her voice faltered. She didn't finish, and he didn't press her. Instead, he took a deep breath, letting the hurt settle into something quieter, colder. He knew then that the damage had already been done, the fracture in their relationship deepened beyond repair.

Without another word, he turned and walked out of the room, leaving her standing in the doorway, a silent figure framed by the glow of the phone that now held the remnants of their broken marriage.

Valerie swiped through the profiles, each one more disappointing than the last. Men complaining about ex-wives, emotional baggage, or unhealed wounds from their past relationships. None of them seemed to offer the fresh start she'd been hoping for, none of them seemed any different from David—just another set of fractured lives trying to piece themselves together. She felt a pang of regret, one she hadn't expected. Trading David had seemed like a simple solution to the discontent she'd carried for so long, but now, faced with these faceless strangers, she wondered if the real problem was her. Maybe it wasn't David who was broken. Maybe it was her own expectations, her need for something more, something that didn't exist.

The app buzzed again. Another notification.

This time, it wasn't a man's profile but a message. Her heart skipped, thinking it might be David—some kind of last-minute reconciliation. But it wasn't him. It was just a reminder from NEXT, an impersonal prompt asking her to rate her "post" experience, to offer feedback on the trade process. She dropped her phone on the table, rubbing her temples. How had she come to this? Her life, once filled with so much promise, had become a blur of poor decisions, each one leading her further from the person she thought she wanted to be. She had traded David for the idea of freedom, but now that freedom felt empty, like a room with no walls. Her thoughts drifted back to their last conversation, the finality of the silence that hung between them when he left. It wasn't anger or bitterness she felt now—it was exhaustion. The kind of tiredness that runs so deep you wonder if you'll ever be able to feel rested again.

Her phone buzzed again, this time a new notification from the app. She hesitated before picking it up, her fingers cold against the screen.

It was a match. A man had swiped on her profile.

Her heart didn't race. There was no excitement, no thrill. Just a quiet resignation.

She tapped the notification, her eyes scanning the profile. Another man with a list of complaints about the women he'd been with. Another shadow, just like her. But this time, something shifted. She wasn't looking for someone to save her anymore. She wasn't even sure she was looking for someone at all. She was just… tired. And so, as the rain continued to tap against the window, Valerie put her phone down. She stared at it for a long moment, the words on the screen blurring into the same gray haze as the world outside. She wasn't ready to make a choice. Not yet. Not when it felt like everything had already been decided for her. Maybe, for now, she needed to find a way to be alone. To learn how to exist in the silence before she could ever be ready to invite someone else into her life.

The irony of it all stung more than the wine. She'd thought listing David would be her way out—a clean break, a fresh start. Yet here she was, staring down a line of profiles that reflected her own struggles back at her, each man's flaws amplifying her own insecurities. It was as if NEXT was mocking her, forcing her to confront all the things she'd tried to escape by throwing David to the wolves first.

She took another sip, the liquid warmth doing little to numb the shame creeping up her spine. She'd been so certain this would liberate her from the life that had become a prison, but instead, the experience had only heightened her loneliness, her discontent. How had she convinced herself that strangers would bring her peace when she couldn't find it within her own walls? Valerie glanced at her phone, the screen now dimmed, the image of Jack's profile burned into her mind.

Her phone buzzed again. She'd left her notifications on, too stubborn to mute them, hoping for a miracle that never came. She picked up the device, barely glancing at the profile that popped up.

"Jack, 43, Local," it read. His list of negative traits was long and blunt: "Ex-convict. Chronic unemployment. History of anger management issues. Known to disappear for days at a time."

This wasn't what she'd wanted, and yet, in a way, it was exactly what she'd signed up for: raw exposure, brutal honesty, and the cold truth about what she'd become in the eyes of others. She wasn't just angry at David; she was angry at herself, angry at the choices that led her here, to this moment of bitter clarity.

She set down her wine, its comfort no longer enough to drown out the gnawing thought that maybe, just maybe, she'd have to face herself before she could move forward. And that, more than the app or David's departure, was what truly terrified her. As she downed another glass, the warmth turned bitter, offering a fleeting numbness that quickly faded, leaving her feeling emptier than before. The house had become a reflection of her inner turmoil—dishes piled up in the sink, clothes strewn about, and a general disarray that only underscored her unraveling. She knew the kids sensed it, and the thought gnawed at her, a guilt so profound it was nearly unbearable. The notifications from NEXT kept coming, a relentless reminder of her perceived inadequacy, her loneliness. Each time her phone buzzed, she felt herself grow more resentful—toward David, toward the app, but mostly toward herself. She *had* signed up for this, thinking it would empower her, but instead, it had thrown her deepest insecurities into harsh relief. She looked over at her youngest, a child barely old enough to speak, who was now clumsily trying to console her with a mismatched hug, sticky fingers patting her back with innocent concern. The sight made her throat tighten. These kids, her kids, were the only constants she had, and yet here she was, slipping further away from them each day. Somewhere in the depths of her despair, a small voice fought to break through, urging her to step back, to re-evaluate, to find a way to pick herself up. Valerie closed her eyes, taking a slow, shaky breath. She couldn't change the past—couldn't take back the choices that had brought her here. But perhaps, she thought, as the kids lingered nearby, she still had a chance to change her future, for them if not for herself. It was a tiny glimmer, but in her fractured world, it was something.

The phone buzzed again, and she reluctantly picked it up. This time, a profile for a man named Ray filled her screen. His profile picture was grainy, but his face was hard, his eyes holding a mean glint. She scrolled to his description, her heart sinking as she read.

"Ray, 39, Occasional Employment. History of violence. Currently on probation. Looking for a stable partner, open-minded about kids."

The last line felt like a slap. She put her phone down, her hands shaking. This was her "match"? She thought about her children upstairs, about the sacrifices she'd made for them. She'd wanted a better life, a way out of the exhausting cycle she'd been trapped in, but the NEXT system was handing her a man who seemed far more dangerous than David ever was.

Valerie felt her stomach twist as she stared at Ray's profile. This wasn't what she'd imagined when she'd posted

David, hoping for a chance at something—anything—better. She had expected an upgrade, someone who could provide her with stability, perhaps even a spark of the companionship she so desperately missed. But the men appearing in her matches seemed only to mirror her own despair back at her, offering little but the same brokenness she was trying to escape. She set the phone down and closed her eyes, the weight of her choices settling heavily on her shoulders. What had she been thinking, putting her life on display for strangers to judge? The app had been a tempting escape, a door she thought would lead to something brighter. But instead, it had only forced her to confront the reality she'd spent years avoiding. Her kids' laughter drifted down the stairs, breaking through her thoughts. She stood up, crossing to the window and watching the rain drizzle in thin, steady lines down the glass. She remembered a time when she'd found joy in the simple moments with her family, even with all their struggles. Maybe that was where her focus needed to be—not on trying to trade one broken relationship for another, but on repairing the life she already had.

With a sigh, she picked up her phone, her thumb hesitating over the app's delete button. It would mean giving up on her idea of a fresh start, of some knight-in-shining-armor stepping in to rescue her. But as she looked around her cluttered living room, she felt a sliver of clarity. Perhaps the person she needed to rely on wasn't waiting out there on a screen—it was her, right here, facing her reality, for her kids and for herself. Taking a deep breath, Valerie pressed the delete button, feeling a quiet sense of relief wash over her as the app disappeared from her screen. It wasn't a solution, but it was a step forward. The message sat on her screen like a ticking bomb, each word pressing down on her.

Ray has shown interest in your profile.

She stared at it, feeling her pulse quicken and her hands begin to shake. She knew she couldn't ignore it—she'd opened this door, invited this chaos in with her own actions. And now, it was coming back to haunt her. In her mind, she tried to justify it all, the spiraling choices, the hopeless search for something better. She'd only wanted a way out of the monotony, a life that felt more than just scraping by. But now, the price of her desperation was staring her down with a violence she hadn't bargained for. Swallowing hard, she forced herself to close the notification, her heart hammering as she wrestled with what to do next. She felt an overwhelming urge to delete her profile, to erase herself from the NEXT system entirely. But a small, self-destructive part of her hesitated, keeping her hand from swiping away the app. How had it come to this—relying on a flawed, faceless algorithm to match her with someone she didn't even know, all in the name of a fresh start? Valerie closed her eyes, trying to steady herself. She needed to get a grip, needed to pull back from this edge she'd put herself on. This wasn't just about her anymore. She had her kids upstairs, each one counting on her to keep things together. It was time to let go of the fantasy of being "rescued" and face her own life, no matter how imperfect. She powered off her phone, set it down, and exhaled deeply. It was time to own up to her choices—no more shortcuts, no more running.

David managed a polite nod, adjusting his grip on the duffel bag, though his shoulders felt tight, weighed down by the unspoken expectations crackling in the air between them. Linda extended a hand, her grip firm, the sort that seemed to signal control rather than warmth.

"David, right? I'm Linda. Welcome to Ridgeville," she said, voice clipped yet rehearsed, as if she'd said these same words to countless others before him.

"Yeah, David," he replied, trying to keep his voice steady despite the odd, hollow sensation in his chest. He'd barely processed the last few days, how everything had unraveled so fast with Valerie, and now here he was, in this bleak little town, a stranger in someone else's life.

As they walked to the parking lot, he noticed Linda glancing at him every few steps, eyes narrowed as though she were dissecting him with each look. He felt the old defense mechanisms kick in, the part of him that knew how to put on a show, say the right things, play the role expected of him. Yet, somehow, that felt exhausting even before they'd reached her car. The silence between them was broken only by the crunch of gravel underfoot, punctuated by an occasional remark from Linda about the "quaint charm" of the town, a charm that was apparently lost on David. Each step closer to her car felt like another weight added to the pile.

Once they reached her modest sedan, Linda unlocked it, gesturing for him to put his bag in the trunk.

"So," she began as they settled in and she started the engine, "I assume you read my profile?" She kept her eyes on the road, hands gripping the wheel with an intensity that matched the tension radiating off her.

David hesitated, unsure how honest he should be. The truth was, he'd barely looked at her profile. He hadn't been prepared for any of this—the move, the trade, the idea that his life could be dismantled and reassembled in some unfamiliar place with someone he didn't know.

"Yeah," he replied, feigning casual interest. "I read it." The words tasted bitter, and he hoped she wouldn't press for details.

Their drive to her house was short, yet the silence stretched uncomfortably between them. David tried to start a conversation, something casual to break the tension, but Linda kept her responses short, clipped. She seemed polite enough, but there was a rigidity to her that made him feel like he was the unwanted guest at a dinner party rather than her new partner. Her house was spacious, a little too immaculate. Every surface was spotless, every item precisely placed. It felt more like a museum than a home, sterile and uninviting, with shelves lined with books sorted by size and color, art arranged in measured symmetry, and not a single piece of clutter in sight. The floors gleamed, and David caught himself hesitating at the entrance, not wanting to track in even a single speck of dirt. Linda stepped inside ahead of him, her heels clicking on the polished wood floors, and motioned him in with a brief nod. She didn't even glance back to see if he followed, her focus already shifting to the thermostat on the wall, which she adjusted with a quick flick.

"Shoes off, please," she said over her shoulder, her tone brisk but not unkind.

David slipped off his shoes, setting them neatly by the door, already feeling like he was intruding in some unspoken, orderly world that had no place for imperfections—or for him, if he wasn't careful. He looked around, taking in the sparse decor, the cold elegance of the space. The silence in the house was overwhelming, punctuated only by the faint hum of the heating system.

"Nice place," he offered, though it sounded hollow, even to his own ears.

Linda nodded, her eyes following his gaze, but there was no pride in her expression, just the same scrutinizing detachment she'd had since the airport. "It suits my needs," she replied, voice flat. "I like things a certain way."

David felt his mouth go dry. This was a far cry from the chaos of home, where the kids' toys were scattered around and Valerie was always one step behind in a battle to keep everything from falling apart. Here, there was no hint of warmth, no sign of a life lived with messes, laughs, or mistakes.

Linda finally turned to face him. "I have a room set up for you," she said, gesturing down the hall. "It's small but should be adequate for your needs."

He followed her down the hallway, noticing that even the art on the walls was arranged with an exactness that felt almost military. She opened a door at the end of the hall, revealing a compact bedroom. It was simple, clean, just like the rest of the house, with a neatly made bed, a small dresser, and a closet that looked like it had barely been used.

"I don't keep much company," she said, her tone making it clear that he was more an occupant than a welcomed guest.

David managed a small nod, stepping inside and setting his bag on the bed. He watched as Linda lingered in the doorway, her gaze flicking around the room as if checking for anything out of place. When she seemed satisfied, she gave him a curt nod and turned to leave.

"Dinner's at six," she said over her shoulder. "Punctuality is… appreciated."

David felt the weight of her unspoken rules settling on him like a heavy coat. This wasn't just a fresh start; it was a new prison, complete with invisible bars and a rigid warden.

Linda turned to him with that unrelenting smile, extending a printed sheet of paper. "These are the house rules," she said. "I like to run things in an orderly way here, so I expect you to follow them exactly."

David took the sheet, glancing at the list. The words blurred for a moment as he processed what he was looking at: a meticulously detailed list of rules, each one itemized and bullet-pointed. It read like something out of a boarding school or a military academy rather than a set of boundaries for a romantic partnership.

"No shoes in the living room. Bedtime is at 10:30 p.m. sharp. No loud noises after 8 p.m. Toilet seat must be left down. Use coasters at all times. Dishes must be washed and dried immediately after each meal. No visitors without prior approval. Text when you're going to be late…" The list went on.

David looked up, his mouth halfway open, searching for words that might defuse the unease churning in his stomach. He managed a weak laugh. "You, uh, really like order, huh?"

Her smile didn't falter. "I've found that people function best with structure," she replied evenly. "Without it, relationships fall apart. NEXT has shown me that consistency is key. David, if we're going to make this work, you need to understand that my system is non-negotiable."

David lay still, feeling as if even the slightest movement might shatter the silence and bring Linda's strict orderliness down on him. He couldn't shake the sense of entrapment, the feeling that he was wedged into a life that wasn't his, one dictated by rules that left no room for warmth or humanity.

A dozen regrets churned in his mind, colliding with flickers of resentment and frustration. He'd never imagined that agreeing to NEXT would lead to this—trapped in a pristine, lifeless house, bound to someone who saw him more as a fixture than a partner. The thought of enduring this for an entire year made his stomach knot. He closed his eyes, attempting to push it all away, but the reality clung to him, sinking deeper with each passing moment. His mind drifted to Valerie and the life he'd left behind. Their marriage had been far from perfect, but there was at least something real beneath the chaos—a connection, however frayed, that had been forged over years of shared struggles and fleeting moments of joy. Here, all he felt was a gnawing hollowness, as if he'd traded every imperfect but genuine part of his past for a meticulously crafted illusion of a relationship. Just as he felt himself slipping into a restless sleep, Linda stirred, muttering something under her breath before settling back down. David let out a slow breath, wishing that he could muster the strength to find a way out, but knowing, for now, he was bound to this sterile, hollow life by a commitment he wasn't sure he could honor.

David sat up in bed, the frustration twisting his insides, harder to ignore with each passing minute. The faint light from the digital clock on Linda's bedside table cast an eerie glow over the rule sheet resting beside it. The words were crisply printed, and somehow, that made them even more oppressive, as though the ink itself was mocking him for thinking he could escape this rigid new life.

Linda's breathing was slow and steady, completely at peace in her world of rules and routines, unaffected by the trap they'd both willingly stepped into. He almost envied her sense of satisfaction, her ability to take comfort in the structure of things. She'd likely set up her life exactly as she wanted it: immaculate, precise, governed by rules and boundaries that gave her control. He could see now that she hadn't chosen him for companionship, but as a piece to fit into her meticulously designed puzzle. He'd been exchanged like a pawn in this game of emotional bartering, both of them unknowingly manipulated by the faceless entity that was NEXT. And here he was, bound by a contract as unforgiving as Linda's perfectly polished floors, forbidden from escaping until a year of this "serious, committed attempt" had passed. He was starting to understand the full extent of NEXT's power—not just the matchmaking itself, but the complete psychological control it exerted. It didn't take away freedom in the usual sense, but it offered an illusion of choice, only to lock people down with terms and conditions no one could fully grasp until they were trapped. The fine print had seemed simple when he'd signed up; he'd been too distracted by his own bitterness and disappointment to see the hooks buried within it.

David let his gaze wander across the shadowed room, taking in the signs of Linda's meticulous nature. Everything was lined up, color-coded, and arranged with a strict symmetry that left no room for deviation. It was as though she'd smoothed out every imperfection in her home, as if purging messiness from her environment could somehow keep it at bay in her life. This place wasn't a home—it was a gallery of rules, and each rule represented a concession he'd have to make, a part of himself he'd need to silence if he was going to survive here. But that word—survive—stuck with him. Was he really willing to just survive? To live in a space so devoid of comfort and warmth, like a stranger forced to follow a script? It seemed absurd, even humiliating, to let himself fall in line, to just "wait out" the year like a prisoner counting down the days of a sentence. That wasn't living. And if he let himself go down that road, he feared he'd lose even the smallest part of himself that was still intact after everything that had gone wrong with Valerie. The rules he was forced to follow weren't just Linda's—they were NEXT's as well. In fact, NEXT had set the parameters for everything, creating a binding expectation that he'd conform, adapt, and eventually settle. It wasn't just about matching people based on mutual dissatisfaction; it was about breaking them down until they couldn't imagine life without the board, until they accepted that being reshuffled like inventory was better than being alone. And that, David realized with a sickening jolt, was what he resented the most.

David's pulse quickened as he considered his options. If he broke the contract, NEXT would put him back on the board, and the cycle would start again with someone new— another stranger with a list of unmet needs and unresolved issues. But what if he refused to play by the rules? What if he could find a way out that didn't mean just switching partners, but breaking free of the whole system? He didn't know if it was even possible, but for the first time, he felt something other than resignation. A spark of defiance began to flicker inside him, refusing to be smothered by fear. He closed his eyes, breathing deeply, feeling the small pulse of rebellion grow. He'd have to be careful; NEXT wouldn't let him go easily, and he doubted Linda would welcome any disruption to her carefully controlled life. But he couldn't let himself be reduced to a profile on a screen, a commodity traded and judged by strangers. He had let himself be drawn into this by bitterness and desperation, but he didn't have to let it define him. There had to be a way to escape, to break free from the endless cycle of failed connections and secondhand matches. As he lay back down, he felt a strange calm settle over him. He wasn't beaten—not yet. The system wanted him to submit, to settle into the dull rhythm of obligation, but he'd made up his mind. He'd find a way out, no matter what it took. This was his life, and he wasn't going to let anyone, least of all a faceless app, tell him how to live it.

The days drifted into one another, a seamless blur of emptiness punctuated only by the practical demands of her children, whom she met with a weariness that seemed etched into her bones. She couldn't remember the last time she'd felt anything other than numb, dragging herself through each morning with the remnants of last night's wine still swirling in her veins. She'd traded David, expecting some spark of relief or hope, but instead, she was left with a suffocating solitude that felt as unforgiving as the NEXT board she had used against him. The sharp edges of her life softened in the haze, and she slipped further into the bottle as each day passed. Where once she'd told herself it was only to unwind, her evening drinks had spiraled into a crutch—a slow escape from reality. The household slipped into a kind of managed chaos, clutter accumulating in corners, dishes piling high, and laundry left in heaps that seemed to mirror her own tangled state of mind. She shuffled through it all in a near trance, moving just enough to keep the bare minimum running, leaving the older kids to care for the younger ones whenever she fell into bed too early—or too late. One afternoon, she caught sight of herself in the smudged bathroom mirror, her face illuminated by the flat, unkind light above. The woman who stared back seemed hollowed out, a stranger with thinning, messy hair and eyes rimmed with fatigue. The person she saw bore little resemblance to the woman she remembered from a happier time, back when she'd thought life could still be pieced together, when the world hadn't seemed so unyielding, and she hadn't yet felt trapped in the echo of her own mistakes.

A part of her—a voice that surfaced only when the numbing effects of alcohol wore thin—began to question the cost of all this. The small moments of resentment, the petty decisions, the years she had lost clinging to the illusion of revenge or control…had it all only served to dig her deeper into this pit? The weight of her own choices pressed heavily on her, and for the first time in years, she wondered if there might be a way to turn things around. But the thought was fleeting, drowned in the familiar haze that had become her refuge. Each notification felt like a slow descent into humiliation, each name another reminder of the misstep that had spiraled her life into this unyielding cycle.

She'd swipe them away in disgust, but they always returned, each message more desperate than the last. The profiles were disheartening—gritty, haphazard snapshots of men with vacant eyes, their faces set in grim expressions that mirrored the resignation she felt in her own soul. Some messaged her directly, treating her not as a person, but as an object—an escape, a temporary fix to their own hollow loneliness.

One afternoon, a sense of desperation washed over her, cutting through the familiar fog. She opened the app, this time with a real plan: she would delete her account, wipe her profile clean, and leave this system that had trapped her in a relentless cycle of despair. She scrolled frantically through the settings, her fingers trembling as she searched for any option that might let her disappear from the app once and for all.

Instead, she was met with the message she dreaded:

"Unable to remove user from the system until a match is finalized."

The words felt like a slap. They stared back at her in unyielding, stark text, unblinking and unsympathetic. The app was her jailer, cold and unfeeling, reminding her that escape was impossible without another "successful" match. It was an endless loop, designed to keep people cycling through partners, bonded not by connection or compatibility, but by shared resignation. In this system, it seemed she was no more than a profile, a transaction, waiting for someone—anyone—to claim her.

With a bitter laugh, she closed the app, tossing the phone aside as if it burned her. She was no closer to freedom than she had been before. The irony wasn't lost on her: in trying to trade David for a fresh start, she'd only chained herself to something far darker and more isolating. The emptiness gnawed at her, louder than ever now that she realized there was truly no way out.

She sank into the couch, feeling the familiar pull toward the half-finished wine bottle nearby. But this time, the feeling tasted different—harsher, colder.

"You've received a message from Curtis: Your perfect match awaits you."

For a long moment, she just stared at the screen, her pulse pounding in her ears, her vision blurring slightly from the alcohol. She wanted to dismiss it as just another empty promise, but something about the message sent a chill down her spine.

Ready to do what it takes.

The words were bold, almost taunting. In the dim glow of her phone screen, they seemed to stand out, leaving an unsettling weight in the pit of her stomach. Against her better judgment, she clicked on his profile, trying to learn more. But Curtis's page was nearly blank—a single, blurry silhouette as his profile picture, with no personal details, no history, nothing that might hint at who he really was. It felt off, even for NEXT's low standards. Yet there was something insidious about the emptiness, a vacuum where a person's life should have been.

A sense of unease began to grow in her, prickling at her skin, but she pushed it down, chalking it up to her own paranoia and the whiskey clouding her mind. Still, the dread lingered, sharp and unyielding. She put her phone down, tossing it onto the coffee table, as if putting physical distance between herself and Curtis's message might lessen the fear creeping into her bones. But his words echoed in her mind, circling her thoughts like a dark shadow she couldn't shake. Valerie took another long sip from the whiskey bottle, hoping to drown the feeling, yet it only amplified her hollow ache. She had thought she could find someone better, a glimmer of hope that had pulled her into the NEXT cycle, yet here she was—stranded, haunted by her own choices, and taunted by the ghost of a life she had willingly dismantled. Curling up on the couch, Valerie felt the overwhelming weight of loneliness settle over her. She thought of her children asleep upstairs, blissfully unaware of the chaos their mother was sinking into. She knew they needed her, deserved more than what she'd become, yet she felt powerless to climb out of the mess she'd made. The night stretched on, dark and still, and she drifted in and out of fitful sleep. Curtis's words echoed through her dreams, chilling her with their promise and their threat, until she finally drifted off completely, clutching the empty bottle like it was the only anchor she had left in the world.

CHAPTER THREE

The cracks in the system were impossible to ignore, even as the corporate machine behind NEXT continued to tout its success. On paper, the system had "reduced" the divorce rate, but it had also morphed into a grotesque parody of itself. Relationships no longer had the chance to breathe and grow naturally. Instead, they were accelerated, forced into premature pairings based on a list of faults and flaws, leaving little room for genuine connection or healing. As the months passed, stories started to surface. Some came from people trapped in these mismatched unions who had been relegated to living with strangers who shared none of their values, interests, or even a basic level of kindness. Others came from those who had endured the soul-crushing experience of being "re-listed" after their first attempt at a relationship failed under the weight of unmet expectations. Many of them were individuals who had believed the NEXT system would grant them a new start, only to find themselves shackled to someone who, despite the glowing promises of compatibility, turned out to be just another person with a history of pain, trauma, or dysfunction. The couples who remained in the system, whether they liked it or not, were left battling their own internal demons. With no time for reflection or emotional recovery, the forced partnerships began to deteriorate quickly. Arguments over trivial things escalated into violent confrontations, and resentment simmered beneath the surface, threatening to boil over at any moment. Domestic violence became rampant, a shocking but predictable result of putting people together who hadn't been given the chance to heal or truly understand one another. Trust was obliterated, replaced by suspicion and anger. These incidents were not rare—they became a daily occurrence, swept under the rug by the NEXT system's public relations machine, which continued to paint a rosy picture of perfect matches and happy families. Behind the scenes, though, the toll was undeniable. The casualties were emotional and psychological, their scars hidden beneath a glossy façade. People had been promised a second chance at love and happiness, but instead, they were stuck in a broken system that perpetuated their suffering, one flawed pairing after another. The consequences reached further than just the couples involved. Children, caught in the crossfire of these broken relationships, were left confused and anxious, unable to understand the dynamic shift from their parents' previous relationships. Those who had been thrust into a new family under the NEXT system were left to navigate their own emotional turmoil, often feeling like pawns in a game they didn't understand.

In the streets, at local schools, in grocery stores— whispers of discontent grew louder. People began to question the legitimacy of the system. The question wasn't whether NEXT had failed them—it was how long they could continue living in its shadow before it consumed them entirely. But the worst part was how difficult it had become to escape. Once paired, individuals were locked into contracts, forced to give the relationship a "serious, committed attempt" before they could even think about being re-listed. And when they were eventually paired again, it wasn't with someone who understood them or cared for them. No—NEXT treated them like used commodities, each fresh pairing a reminder of how little agency they had left in their own lives. The idea of a happy ending seemed increasingly like a distant dream. The NEXT system had promised people freedom, the chance to move beyond their past relationships, but in reality, it had only shackled them to a never-ending cycle of false hope and deepening despair.

Trevor Kline sat in his office, staring at the thick stack of reports in front of him. The numbers didn't lie, but they didn't tell the full story, either. He had been an ardent supporter of NEXT from the beginning, the one who had championed it as the answer to a broken system. It had promised a world where relationships were more efficient, more sustainable, where people could escape the crushing weight of toxic marriages and false starts. But now, as he sifted through the flood of alarming statistics, Trevor couldn't shake the feeling that he had been complicit in something far darker than he had ever imagined. Divorce rates had dropped, yes, but what they didn't account for was the wave of silent suffering that had taken its place. Mental health professionals were overwhelmed, their resources stretched to the breaking point, and emergency intervention teams were racing to respond to the ever-growing tide of calls for domestic violence and attempted suicides. People who had once trusted in the system were now left grappling with feelings of isolation, hopelessness, and betrayal. What was supposed to be a hopeful new beginning had turned into a suffocating trap. It was as if the system had created a factory line for human misery, each flawed pairing producing more brokenness than the last. Trevor's own sense of guilt had been creeping up on him slowly, then all at once. He had sat in boardrooms, hearing pitches, signing off on plans, all while convinced they were doing the right thing. But now, as he looked at the faces of the people he'd once believed were helped by NEXT, he couldn't help but feel responsible for the hurt they were enduring. There was no way to ignore the testimonies of those who had been paired with individuals they had no connection with, no way to ignore the increase in calls to therapy centers, where patients didn't just seek help for personal trauma—they sought help because the very fabric of their relationships had been ripped apart by a system that prioritized matching flaws over fostering genuine compatibility.

The reports he was reading detailed a rise in emotional manipulation, coercion, and even violence. Many couples—who had been placed in these forced partnerships—felt trapped by the system's rules. The threat of being re-listed was often enough to keep people in relationships that were psychologically damaging, afraid of facing the public shame of a failed pairing. Some were coerced into staying in toxic, volatile situations, believing they had no choice but to "make it work" for the sake of their future. But for those who had already endured personal trauma, the weight of a forced relationship could break them, causing mental breakdowns, spirals into addiction, and even worse.

Trevor ran his hand through his hair, frustration boiling over. He had trusted the algorithm, the people behind it, and the idea that the system could provide people with second chances at love and stability. But now, he was forced to confront the fact that the system had become the very thing it was supposed to fix. He thought back to his first meeting with the founders, when they had spoken with such confidence about the potential of NEXT to revolutionize relationships. How naïve he had been. His phone buzzed, pulling him from his thoughts. It was an alert from one of the crisis intervention centers—a report of another violent incident involving two individuals paired through NEXT. He sighed, rubbed his temples, and clicked through the message. There was no end in sight. The problems were stacking up faster than the system could keep up with, and the public's faith in the program was eroding with each passing day.

Trevor knew something had to change. He couldn't ignore it any longer. The very program he had helped build was now a breeding ground for pain, and if he didn't act soon, the consequences would only grow more severe. The question was: How could he stop it? How could he unravel the very thing he had helped create, without causing even more damage in the process? As he stood up from his desk, the weight of the decision settled on him like a heavy cloak. He had no answers—only questions. But for the first time, he wasn't sure he could live with the answers NEXT had provided.

The more Trevor dug, the more the horror set in. He'd once thought of the algorithm as a neutral tool—a scientific approach to matchmaking that would bypass human error and bias. But what he found now was a stark, unsettling truth: the algorithm didn't understand the nuances of human behavior. It wasn't equipped to separate those seeking genuine connection from those harboring harmful patterns. Instead, it treated every participant as a statistical input, a data point to be paired with another in a web of traits, quirks, and flaws without any real grasp of the human consequences. Trevor took meticulous notes as he went through each case, feeling the weight of his own complicity bear down on him. The stories he read were raw and painful, the voices behind them cracking under the strain of trauma. One man described how he'd been matched repeatedly with women who displayed severe trust issues due to prior abuse. His own history of mental health struggles had been reduced to a checkbox labeled "low tolerance for conflict." The system interpreted this as a "complementary trait" to partners with volatile emotional needs. The result? A series of disastrous, hurtful relationships that had nearly broken him.

He spoke to a woman named Laura who had fought her way out of a damaging pairing after a grueling three years. She'd been matched with a man who had "anger management issues"—a fact the system had simply labeled as "passionate demeanor." Laura's testimony was chilling. She described how the match had devolved into a cycle of control and intimidation, and when she'd appealed to NEXT to be reassigned, they'd dismissed her claims.

"He just needs understanding," they'd replied. The phrase haunted Trevor as he read, a cruel irony twisting his stomach.

The algorithm's supposed impartiality was, in fact, a cold disregard for the realities of people's lives. It didn't account for trauma or for the ways people could hurt each other. It merely balanced scales of perceived flaws and assigned value based on who could "tolerate" whom. Determined to make a difference, Trevor began contacting other members of the board, hoping to push for a serious reform. He knew he'd face resistance—after all, the system was profitable, and no one liked to admit they'd made a grievous error. But Trevor wasn't interested in preserving reputations or profits anymore. He was intent on exposing the failings of NEXT and advocating for those it had hurt.

As he clicked through email threads and filed documents, his phone buzzed with a new alert: a report on another violent incident, this one involving a recent trade where a woman had been matched with her partner's former abuser. Trevor's hands clenched as he read the details. The system had overlooked the man's previous record because of its policy of second chances, assuming every trade was a fresh start rather than a continuation of a dangerous cycle.

Trevor couldn't stand it any longer. He had been a silent enabler in the machine that was systematically breaking people. The system's promise of a perfect match was nothing more than a shallow slogan masking the reality of suffering behind closed doors. It was time to take action—to dismantle this system he'd once championed and give people the choice they'd been denied.

As Trevor navigated the back-end of the system, his screen lit up with hidden files and encrypted pathways he hadn't even known existed. Each file he opened was a testament to the twisted priorities of NEXT's creators. He discovered documentation on the algorithm's "Compatibility Deviation" function, which intentionally paired users marked as vulnerable or high-need with individuals deemed emotionally stable but unlikely to leave due to financial or social circumstances. These weren't partnerships—they were codependent traps. The algorithm preyed on people's weakest moments, ensuring a steady flow of trades that lined the pockets of investors. Another layer revealed an even darker truth: profiles flagged for low self-esteem, depression, or emotional trauma were assigned higher match probabilities with others who displayed controlling or manipulative traits. The idea was to create a dependence cycle, the system banking on the anchor effect—a psychological phenomenon where people are more likely to stay in dysfunctional relationships due to perceived scarcity of options. In NEXT's case, the algorithm reinforced the feeling of scarcity, making each user feel that if this match didn't work out, their prospects were slim to none.

Trevor's blood ran cold. This wasn't a flaw in the algorithm—it was deliberate, calculated. The system fed on desperation, knowing that these cycles would not only keep users engaged but also bolster statistics. The NEXT team could claim that fewer people were single or filing for divorce, but in reality, they were shackling individuals to toxic dynamics in a prison with invisible walls. He stumbled across emails between higher-ups, laughing off user complaints as isolated incidents. One message casually dismissed a complaint about abuse, suggesting the dissatisfied user simply wasn't trying hard enough." Another included a chilling line from a high-ranking developer. "People are commodities, not customers. We aren't selling happiness. We're selling retention."

The scope of betrayal Trevor felt was overwhelming. He'd once believed in this project, driven by the naive hope that technology could solve human issues. But this wasn't about solving problems—it was about creating them. As he scanned the files, a thought surfaced in his mind: if he could access these files, he could leak them. It would be a whistleblower move, one that could dismantle his entire career, but at this point, it was a risk he was willing to take.

With a steely resolve, Trevor began downloading the files to an encrypted drive, the weight of his decision heavy but strangely empowering. He no longer cared about NEXT's image or his own. The only thing that mattered now was stopping this machine from destroying more lives.

Trevor stared at the data with a mixture of dread and disgust as the test batch confirmed his worst fears. The algorithm wasn't just flawed—it was predatory, engineered to capitalize on pain. Profiles flagged for trauma were consistently matched with individuals who had a history of dominance or manipulation, pairing desperation with control as if human connection could be distilled into a clinical, mechanical outcome. Stability, as defined by the algorithm, had nothing to do with compatibility or mutual support. Instead, it was about keeping people locked in dysfunctional loops that made them unlikely to question the system or to leave. As the lines of code ran through his screen, he could see precisely how the algorithm evaluated matches: high-risk factors like addiction or emotional dependency increased a user's likelihood of being matched with someone equally trapped in their own misery or with someone who could easily exploit their vulnerabilities. Trevor felt sick as he realized this wasn't an accident or oversight but a meticulously crafted model. The architects of NEXT had prioritized user engagement metrics over real connections, believing that broken people were more likely to cling to whatever semblance of stability the system could offer.

With each result, his horror grew. The test revealed that those with a history of trauma were cycled through ideal matches that would supposedly stabilize them, but in truth, only deepened their sense of isolation and despair. By consistently placing vulnerable individuals into damaging relationships, NEXT was ensuring that people stayed reliant on the app, feeding into the cycle of dependence. He imagined all the people he had unknowingly condemned to this algorithm, trusting blindly in the system's promises. The faces of countless couples flashed through his mind, people he had thought were finding solace in new beginnings but who were actually being funneled into calculated traps.

Trevor's hands hovered over the keyboard. This system needed to be dismantled, but taking it down wouldn't be easy. The data he'd uncovered was a powerful weapon, but wielding it would pit him against not just NEXT, but a network of corporate interests too invested in its success. A quiet resolve settled over him—whatever it took, he would find a way to expose this machine for the nightmare it was. As Trevor paced the cold, sterile office, the weight of his decision settled heavily on his shoulders. Every detail of the system he once trusted now felt like a trap he'd set for the very people he'd sworn to help. He'd pitched NEXT as a way to mend broken hearts and rebuild stability in people's lives, yet the brutal math he'd just witnessed revealed an entirely different purpose. People weren't healing; they were being hollowed out, fractured deeper with each forced match, each time the system recycled their pain. He glanced at his phone, tempted to call someone—anyone who could confirm he wasn't the only one feeling this way. But he knew that speaking to the wrong person, or even confiding in the right one, could spell disaster before he'd had a chance to do anything. The board had invested heavily in NEXT, and they wouldn't hesitate to shut him down if they caught wind of what he was about to do. In their eyes, he wasn't a whistleblower—he was a liability.

Taking a deep breath, Trevor returned to his computer and began documenting everything he had found. He saved copies of data reports, screenshots of flagged complaints, and even testimonies that showed clear patterns of abuse and coercion within matches. He knew he needed a record, something ironclad, that could stand against the inevitable storm of denial and dismissal he'd face. Exposing NEXT meant putting every last scrap of evidence into the open. But a plan was one thing—execution was another. Trevor would have to act fast, and alone. And, he realized, he'd need help from people who understood the reality of the system firsthand. Valerie. David. If anyone could provide the stories, the real experiences that would make the public understand the devastation NEXT had caused, it was them.

He pushed away the rising panic. This wasn't just about risking his career. This was about facing the full weight of the destruction he'd helped unleash.

Trevor glanced down at the screen, his fingers hovering over the keyboard. A part of him, the part that had been indoctrinated into believing in the system's potential, screamed for him to stop. But deep down, he knew that to ignore the truth now would make him just as guilty as the others who had enabled this broken system.

He hit "Send."

The notification flashed on his screen:

You have discovered a hidden flaw in the NEXT system. Action required.

Trevor's stomach churned. The countdown had begun.

CHAPTER FOUR

The realization gnawed at Valerie, tugging at her every waking thought. She had no options left; she was trapped in a twisted game with no exit unless she played by NEXT's brutal rules. Days melted into an exhausted blur as she tried to gather herself. She hated what she had done—pushing David out, believing she'd find something better, only to be left stranded with nothing but regrets. Meanwhile, her kids kept their distance, their small voices fading in the background as they clung to each other. They were scared, and Valerie felt their unspoken judgment in every glance. Once, she caught her oldest, Emma, looking at her with a mix of pity and anger that stung worse than any words could have. Valerie wanted to tell her kids she was sorry, to promise things would get better, but the words stuck in her throat. Returning to the app became a dreaded ritual, each tap a reminder of her helplessness. She scrolled through the profiles again and again, each new face more bleak than the last. They were just names, data points—each one a person discarded and pushed along by the same relentless algorithm. She saw her own pain reflected back at her in those hollow eyes, each profile as desperate for an escape as she was.

But there was no mercy in NEXT's system. To delete her account, she'd have to select one of these men and commit to the facade of a match. The thought turned her stomach, but she knew she couldn't keep spinning in this cycle forever. Valerie spent sleepless nights, wracked by the thought of diving back in, knowing this might mean entering into yet another miserable pairing. Yet each day her desperation grew, until even the worst options seemed like the only path out of the cage. Eventually, she knew she would have to make a choice, not because she wanted to, but because NEXT had left her no other way. The app felt like a noose tightening around her with every hour, a suffocating reminder that her only escape lay in one final, grueling decision. The message stared back at her, each word on Roger's profile a chilling reminder of the desperate game she was playing. "Interest Shown by Roger W." His name alone seemed innocuous, like the man might be some quiet, ordinary person who posed no threat. But that illusion shattered as she read further, her heart sinking with each new revelation. This wasn't some casual fling or a quick fix—Roger's past painted a picture of a volatile man with a history that screamed danger.

Yet the flicker of a plan formed in Valerie's mind, one tinged with a mix of dread and cold practicality. Maybe she could pair with him temporarily, just long enough to satisfy the system's demands. Once her profile was removed from the NEXT board, maybe, somehow, she could slip out of his life before things took a darker turn. She would disappear, find a loophole in the system's relentless grip, or keep herself scarce long enough that he'd lose interest. It wasn't a great plan; it was barely even a plan at all. But in her cornered mind, it was better than the hell she was living. Anything seemed preferable to the purgatory of waiting, hoping, while knowing the system would never let her go unless she played along. Each option felt tainted, steeped in fear, but if this fragile, flawed strategy could lead to her freedom, even temporarily, it was a risk she had to consider.

Valerie knew it was a gamble—one that could easily backfire. But she was willing to chance it, desperate to believe that she could outmaneuver Roger, NEXT, or anyone who might try to cage her again. Her fingers hovered over the screen as she weighed the risks, the fear clashing with the faint glimmer of hope that this choice, however reckless, might be her one shot at breaking free.

The bar loomed in the distance, a dingy roadside place with flickering neon lights casting a sickly glow over the cracked parking lot. As she pulled in, her stomach twisted tighter, her body caught between the urge to flee and the desperate resolve that had driven her here in the first place. Every instinct screamed to turn around, to abandon this reckless attempt at freedom. But she'd made her choice, and if this was her only way out, she would see it through. She sat in the car for a few long minutes, staring at the entrance, where a handful of patrons lingered, smoking and watching her arrival with casual interest.

Her phone buzzed again.

"Inside. Corner booth."

Roger's message felt like an order, sharp and precise, with no room for negotiation.

Taking a shaky breath, Valerie stepped out of the car, her heels clicking against the uneven asphalt. As she walked into the bar, the dim light inside felt oppressive, making it hard to see anything clearly at first. But then her eyes adjusted, and she saw him.

Roger was hunched in the corner, his gaze fixed on her with an intensity that sent a chill down her spine. His smile was faint, but it reached his eyes—a look of satisfaction, as if she were some long-awaited prize. She approached cautiously, steeling herself as his eyes roamed over her in a way that made her feel stripped and vulnerable. She gave a tight smile, every muscle in her body tense, as if readying herself for whatever came next.

"Valerie," he drawled, motioning for her to sit across from him. His voice was smooth but carried an edge, a hint of something she couldn't quite place but that raised the hairs on the back of her neck. She lowered herself onto the seat, maintaining a rigid posture, her gaze darting around the room, half hoping for an easy escape route that she knew didn't exist.

"I'm glad you showed," he said, leaning forward. "Wasn't sure you would." He gave her another one of those smiles, and she forced herself not to flinch.

She swallowed hard. "I figured I didn't have a choice."

He chuckled softly, his fingers tapping rhythmically on the table. "Good. Honesty is a rare quality these days." He leaned back, his gaze never leaving her, as if assessing her every reaction. The moment stretched, thick with tension, and Valerie felt a heaviness settle over her, the creeping certainty that this was only the beginning of a new nightmare.

All she could do now was play along and hope she found a way out before it was too late.

Valerie forced herself to keep eye contact, masking the dread bubbling inside her. Roger's words carried a weight that left no room for negotiation, his stance radiating a confidence that this meeting was merely a formality in the inevitable course he'd already mapped out. Every instinct screamed at her to turn and run, but her feet felt cemented to the sticky floor.

"I just thought…" she began, her voice barely more than a whisper. "Maybe it would be… easier if we took a little time to adjust." She clung to a slim hope that reasoning might appeal to him, that a glimmer of patience or understanding might exist beneath his cold exterior.

But Roger leaned in closer, his face inches from hers, his eyes glinting with impatience. "This isn't about what you think," he said, his voice low and unyielding. "You said yes. You agreed to the terms. And I'm not the type to waste time."

He took a step back, his eyes scanning her from head to toe as if finalizing his appraisal. "Pack your things and be at my place by the weekend. We're done with this back-and-forth nonsense."

Valerie's heart pounded in her chest, her mind racing through every possible response, every potential way out, but each thought collided with the same unforgiving reality. The system wouldn't release her until she completed this "trade." Roger wasn't someone she could bargain with, and NEXT wasn't something she could outwit.

Trying to hide her fear, she managed a small nod, though she could barely hear her own voice as she muttered, "Fine. The weekend."

He smiled again, satisfied, then pulled out his phone. "Good. I'll text you the address. And don't be late." With that, he turned and walked out, his back straight, his steps confident, as if he'd already won.

The bar felt colder and darker in his absence, but Valerie didn't move. She stared blankly at her hands, which were shaking against the cheap veneer of the table. Her mind echoed with his demands, with the callous certainty that came with them. She hadn't just agreed to a relationship; she'd agreed to a cage. And as she sat there, the reality of her decision settled over her like a prison door slamming shut. If she wanted any chance of escaping the system—and the man it had tied her to—she'd have to find it on her own terms. But for now, all she could do was follow the path laid out in front of her, one unwilling step at a time.

A chill ran through her as his grip bit into her arm, his fingers pressing hard enough to leave bruises. She felt a flash of panic, but forced herself to stay calm, knowing that any sign of fear would only feed his control. The weight of her decision—of hitting "Accept" in a moment of desperation—pressed down on her, trapping her as surely as Roger's grip.

"Roger, please. I just… I just need a little time to get things in order for my kids," she said, her voice steady though her insides churned. She met his gaze, summoning every ounce of strength she had, willing herself to sound unshaken. "I can't uproot them overnight. Give me until the weekend."

His eyes flickered with irritation, but he released her arm, though his expression made it clear this was more a test of her obedience than a concession. "Fine. You have until

Saturday morning. But if you're not there… don't think you can just slip away." His voice dropped, low and dangerous. "I'll make sure you regret it."

As he turned and left, Valerie forced herself to take a deep breath, steadying her shaking hands. She would have to pack up, get her kids ready, and somehow, in the days she had left, find a way out of this nightmare. Every thought seemed a twisted mess of dread, regret, and a frantic, desperate search for a solution. But one thing was clear: she would do anything to protect her children from becoming trapped in the system's cold, unfeeling clutches.

Each night in that sterile room, David felt his spirit shrinking. The walls, painted an unfeeling beige, seemed to close in on him, amplifying the isolation. He couldn't turn on a light without permission, couldn't play music, couldn't so much as rearrange the books on the shelves without enduring Linda's judgmental stare. Every corner of the house bore her rigid, almost militaristic touch, with labels on every drawer and scheduled reminders pinned to the fridge, dictating his every move. It was as if she had mapped out his entire existence to fit her vision of order, with no regard for his autonomy. He'd learned quickly that challenging her rules only made things worse. A hint of resistance, even a small sigh, was enough to earn him a lecture on responsibility and "shared living obligations." He'd tried talking to her, suggesting a compromise or two, but his words were brushed aside like a child's excuse. To

Linda, he wasn't a partner or even an equal; he was an accessory meant to fulfill a role she'd crafted long before he arrived. On the worst nights, when the silence grew too thick to bear, he'd slip a hand under his pillow, clutching the crumpled photo he'd brought from Valerie's place—the one of his kids, their innocent smiles frozen in time. The photo was his only comfort in this cold house, a small piece of the life he'd once known. But even that reminder was painful. He thought of his children's laughter, the messy chaos of their small home, Valerie's loud voice filling every room with complaints and jokes. It had been a flawed, turbulent life, but it was real. It was his.

In Linda's world, he felt like a stranger to himself.

He hovered over the send button, doubting himself. What if this was a trap? What if someone tracked his message and reported him to the authorities, or worse, Linda? But the thought of another day, another hour under her cold, calculating control spurred him on. With a deep breath, he hit "send."

The seconds that followed felt like hours. His pulse hammered as he stared at the screen, waiting for any kind of response. A message popped up, an auto-response perhaps, or maybe just some well-crafted scam: "If you're serious, meet me at Grayson Park, noon sharp. No one else can know. Don't bring your phone." He reread the message three times, half-expecting it to vanish like some fever dream. Grayson Park. The name sent a flicker of familiarity through him. It was miles from Linda's house, a quiet place he used to visit on rare, unsupervised walks. He could imagine its wide-open spaces, the overgrown paths where no one would notice a hurried, private meeting. The thrill of hope surged through him, fragile and electric.

The next morning, David made his preparations. He deleted the chat app and cleared every trace of his message. Paranoia set in as he scanned the room, making sure Linda couldn't see anything unusual. He even had to invent a reason for his absence, throwing on an old, unconvincing smile when Linda questioned him that morning. "I thought I'd get some fresh air, just a walk to stretch my legs," he'd said, swallowing his nerves as she eyed him suspiciously.

Just before noon, David arrived at Grayson Park, heart pounding in his chest. The park was nearly empty, save for a few joggers and a group of elderly women feeding pigeons. He scanned the area, looking for anything—or anyone—that stood out. A figure, hooded and leaning against a tree, caught his eye. The stranger, a wiry man in a faded jacket, looked up, his face obscured beneath a baseball cap. He gave a curt nod, beckoning David over with a slight tilt of his head.

He was told to wait for further communication, and in the days that followed, the messages came—scrambled lines of text, cryptic phrases embedded with hidden meanings, all encrypted and nearly impossible to trace. The senders were unknown, their identities carefully shrouded in secrecy. He could only hope they were who they claimed to be: The Liberators. They were an underground network composed of former lawyers, rogue hackers, and ex-participants who'd managed to slip free of their contracts with NEXT. Some of them had vanished into the shadows with little more than a new name and a borrowed identity, while others had been hidden by powerful connections, people who knew how to keep secrets that could cost lives. The Liberators had a singular purpose—to dismantle the chains of NEXT one escape at a time.

Their plan for him was simple, but not without risk. If he could vanish for a few months, severing all digital traces, the system would eventually categorize him as a "lost asset," flagging his profile as inactive and terminating his binding agreements. But it wouldn't be as easy as just walking away. To vanish meant hiding in plain sight, concealing his movements in a way that would leave nothing behind to track. The thought of freedom drove him, giving him a focus and a purpose he hadn't felt in a long time. Yet David knew that slipping through the cracks of a life under constant scrutiny was a delicate game, one that would require patience, timing, and meticulous planning. Each passing day, Linda's paranoia seemed to sharpen. She watched him with an intensity that bordered on the obsessive, her eyes tracking his every step as if she could sense the thoughts that drifted beneath the surface, an unspoken rebellion brewing within him. Her vigilance seemed to escalate with each subtle shift in his demeanor, as if her instincts told her something was amiss.

Whenever he left the house, even for mundane errands or quick outings, Linda responded by imposing yet another restriction, inventing new ways to tighten the invisible chains that bound him. One day, she revoked his access to the shared car, insisting that it was only fair given his "recent lapses." The next, she locked his access to the home's internal network, claiming it was to avoid any potential for "misunderstandings." Day by day, he felt her grip closing in, each restriction like a wall moving closer, trapping him. His sense of confinement intensified, a creeping claustrophobia seeping into his every thought, making the goal of escape not just a wish but an urgent, desperate need. The thought of liberation lingered at the edge of his mind, flickering like a distant light in an otherwise dark, enclosed room.

One evening, as David stood at the sink, the sound of running water filling the otherwise tense silence, Linda leaned against the counter, watching him with an intensity that made his skin crawl.

She had barely spoken throughout the meal, only to break the silence now, her tone deceptively casual as she said, "I've installed some new cameras around the house."

She smiled, the expression too controlled, the warmth failing to reach her eyes.

"Just for safety," she continued, her voice calm yet carrying a subtle, unspoken threat. "You know how it is—can never be too careful these days, right?"

David forced a nod, trying to steady his breathing. He plastered on a polite smile, one he'd learned to wear often in her presence, though his mind was anything but calm. With every step Linda took to tighten her grip, his anxiety deepened, a current of dread twisting through him. Escape, once a glimmer of hope, seemed to grow fainter as her surveillance increased. The cameras were just another link in the chain, another barrier between him and the outside world. Still, each new restriction fueled a smoldering determination inside him, a resolve that would not be easily extinguished.

As he dried his hands, his phone vibrated in his pocket. Surprised, he glanced at it, catching only a single line of text. It was blunt, chilling: "If you run, they'll find you."

The words sent a jolt through him, a warning that seemed to reach out from the screen and seize him by the throat. His pulse quickened, and for a moment, he found it hard to breathe, the weight of his situation pressing on him like a vise. He could almost picture the faceless agents of NEXT, cold and relentless, tracking him down without hesitation. Linda's watchfulness and these constant warnings only reminded him how the system operated with ruthless precision. If he dared to disappear, Linda would notify them, and the NEXT enforcers—those who ensured compliance with the organization's demands—would pursue him relentlessly. Their methods of punishment were vague yet notorious, spoken of in dark, half-whispered rumors within the underground network. The Liberators had hinted at the consequences, but the details were rarely discussed, as if even saying too much might invite the system's wrath.

Standing there, David felt the full, oppressive power of NEXT, a force that stretched into every aspect of his life, designed to eliminate any thought of defiance. The system wasn't content merely to monitor or limit; it sought to possess, to own those within its reach entirely. He realized that if he faltered, if he hesitated even for a moment, it would seize that weakness, binding him even more tightly than before. But despite the darkness of that warning, despite the terrifying consequences that lay in store, David could not shake his resolve. This was his life, and he could not, would not, surrender it completely. Somewhere within him, the thought of freedom, however distant, however dangerous, remained. He would rather risk everything than allow NEXT to strip him of what little autonomy he had left. His escape plan was set, and he knew it might be his only chance. Even if freedom came at a steep price, David was prepared to pay it, even if it meant leaving behind every comfort, every familiarity. Because in a world dictated by NEXT, freedom was more than a goal—it was the last shred of himself he could hold onto.

Valerie sat in the darkened corner of her living room, the silence pressing in around her as she watched the faint, ghostly shadows flicker across the walls, cast by the dim light from a single lamp. She felt an eerie stillness settle over the room, a quiet made heavier by the presence of Derek, who had fallen asleep on her couch. Or rather, his couch, as he had called it earlier, the words dripping with possessiveness, his tone low and edged with menace. It had only been days since the system had matched them, days since Derek had first stepped over her threshold. Yet in that short span, he had wasted no time staking his claim, moving through her home as though every corner, every piece of furniture, even the very air she breathed, belonged to him. In the beginning, Valerie had held onto a fragile hope, a faint dream that maybe this new match would be different. Maybe, she thought, this time she would find something more—a way out of the monotonous, empty existence that seemed to stretch endlessly before her. She had longed for companionship, for a connection that might bring warmth, laughter, perhaps even love back into her life. But Derek was the antithesis of that dream. His presence seemed to fill the room with a coldness that went deeper than his demeanor, a chill that seeped into her bones. From their very first exchange, he had shown no kindness, only a harshness that felt razor-sharp, an anger that lurked just beneath his gaze, restrained yet ever-present.

It didn't take long for his true nature to slip through the cracks. There was a darkness about him, an edge that sent shivers down her spine. His anger, always simmering just below the surface, had already begun to manifest in ways she could no longer ignore. Small things had set him off—a misplaced item, a noise that interrupted his thoughts—and each time, she had felt his simmering fury fill the air, thick and oppressive. She'd seen the tightening of his jaw, the flash of irritation in his eyes, hints of a dangerous temper lying just below the surface. Her children had felt it too. They sensed the unease, the tension that now lingered in their home, and their instinct had been to retreat, to make themselves as invisible as possible. Her youngest had taken to staying quietly in his room, his laughter now stifled, his once-carefree demeanor replaced by a cautious silence. Her older child, usually protective, had instead gravitated toward his sibling, both of them clinging to each other in a silent alliance, their wide, fearful eyes darting toward her whenever Derek was near. It was as though they had formed their own silent language, communicating their fear without words, their glances heavy with the unspoken understanding that something was wrong.

As Valerie sat there, the reality of her situation loomed over her, stark and undeniable. The man she had let into her life, into her home, was not just incompatible; he was a threat, a looming shadow that darkened her every thought. She could feel herself shrinking in his presence, a helplessness settling over her, blending with a growing terror that clutched at her throat. The dream she'd once held of escaping her own loneliness, of finding someone who might bring light into her life, had twisted into something grotesque, something she no longer recognized. And now, all she wanted was a way out, a way to reclaim her space, her safety, and to shield her children from the man whose anger seemed to taint every room he entered.

It wasn't long before Derek took control in ways that went far beyond mere suggestions. He began to dictate, to command, setting down rules that seemed to seep into every corner of Valerie's life, like an invisible prison closing in. He would tell her what to wear, down to the smallest detail, with criticisms lurking behind every suggestion that didn't align with his preferences. He controlled when she could speak, silencing her with a glare or a lifted hand if her words displeased him, making it clear that his idea of a "partner" was someone who submitted entirely to his will. Each new demand, each imposed restriction, felt like a weight pressing down on her, stifling her sense of self, twisting her reality until she hardly recognized herself. Every time she tried to pull back, to establish some space between them, she would see it—the way his eyes darkened, a storm brewing just below the surface. There was no mistaking the quiet, simmering rage that lingered there, a restrained fury that made her blood run cold. He would laugh, a low, bitter sound that only heightened her sense of dread, mocking her as if her resistance was nothing more than a childish defiance.

"You think you can change your mind now?" he sneered on more than one occasion, a taunting smile twisting his face. "You agreed. You're mine now, and I'm not letting you back out." The words were like chains, binding her in ways she hadn't thought possible, a constant reminder that escape was not an option he would willingly allow.

One evening, after yet another argument whispered in heated tones so as not to wake the children, Valerie retreated to her bedroom, her heart hammering as she shut the door behind her. She sank onto the edge of her bed, her mind racing with desperation, as if every nerve in her body screamed for a solution. With trembling hands, she opened her laptop, feeling a surge of urgency as she began searching for any possible way out, any loophole that might free her from Derek's relentless grip. The screen glowed coldly in the dim light, lines of text swimming before her eyes as she scanned through page after page. But with each line she read, her hope eroded further, replaced by a growing sense of despair. The contract under NEXT was meticulously crafted, a legal fortress designed to trap, not to protect. Every clause, every line seemed to bolster the system's control, leaving no room for personal autonomy. The language was unyielding, airtight. Only in extreme cases—

like death—would the match be nullified, and even then, a participant would be required to re-enroll within a short period. The system treated human lives as data points, numbers to be reallocated without regard for the reality behind them. Nowhere, in any of the meticulously crafted sections, was there mention of safety concerns, nothing to shield individuals from abuse or mistreatment. The NEXT contract operated with a mechanical indifference, blind to the dangers it permitted, as though suffering had no bearing in its clinical calculations.

As she closed her laptop, the despair settled over her like a heavy cloak. She realized, with horrifying clarity, that the system she had once believed in—the one that promised companionship and stability—was not only indifferent to her pain but complicit in it, a silent partner in Derek's control. In that moment, the last vestiges of hope began to slip away, leaving her with a sobering truth: if she wanted to escape Derek's grasp, she would have to find a way to dismantle the very system that had entrapped her. Growing desperate, Valerie scrolled through the NEXT interface, searching for some form of human recourse amid its sterile menus and automated prompts. Finally, she found the number for NEXT's support line. She hesitated before dialing, her hand trembling as her thumb hovered over the call button. It felt absurd to rely on the very system that had ensnared her, but she had no other options. Taking a shaky breath, she pressed the button, the dial tone stretching endlessly before a voice finally picked up on the other end.

"Thank you for contacting NEXT Support. How can we assist you today?"

The voice was soft and measured, disturbingly polite, as if she had called for assistance with a faulty appliance rather than to plead for her safety. It struck a jarring note, the disconnect making her feel even more isolated.

Valerie hesitated, forcing her racing thoughts into coherent words. She knew she couldn't let her emotions spill out unchecked—not if she wanted to be taken seriously.

"I… I need to cancel my match," she began, her voice trembling despite her efforts to sound composed. "My partner, Derek—he's… dangerous. I'm afraid for myself and my children."

There was a pause on the other end, long enough for her pulse to quicken. When the support agent spoke again, their tone was unchanged, a monotone professionalism that felt colder with every word. "I'm sorry to hear about your concerns," they said, as though they were reciting from a script. "However, the NEXT system only permits match cancellations in specific, verifiable cases of violation of the initial terms. Discontent or dissatisfaction is not considered grounds for termination."

Valerie's stomach sank at the clinical detachment in their response. "But this isn't just discontent," she said, her voice cracking as her resolve began to fray. "He's... he's threatened me. I'm scared of what he might do. I can't let my kids live like this, not around someone like him. Please, there has to be something you can do."

Her desperation bled into her words, her plea raw and unfiltered. For a moment, she thought she heard a hint of hesitation in the agent's breath, a flicker of recognition that her situation might warrant more than scripted responses. But when they spoke again, the voice was as measured as before, leaving no room for hope.

"NEXT takes all safety concerns seriously," the agent replied, their tone carefully even. "If you believe your situation involves immediate danger, we recommend contacting local authorities. However, as per the terms of your agreement, NEXT does not arbitrate interpersonal disputes beyond contractual violations." They paused, as if to let their words settle. "Should you feel that Derek has violated the explicit conditions of your match, we encourage you to gather evidence and submit a formal complaint through the proper channels for review."

Valerie's grip on the phone tightened as their words sank in. *Evidence. Formal complaints.* As if her fear and desperation could be quantified into tidy documents, as if she had time to catalog Derek's threats while ensuring her children's safety.

"And what am I supposed to do in the meantime?" she asked, her voice barely above a whisper, the tears she had fought to suppress beginning to break free. "Wait until it's too late?"

The silence on the other end stretched unbearably long. When the agent finally spoke, their tone was unyielding. "I'm sorry, ma'am. Is there anything else we can assist you with today?"

Valerie didn't respond. Her hand fell limp at her side as she ended the call, the hollow beep echoing in the room. She stared at the phone, her heart heavy with the realization that she was on her own. NEXT wasn't just indifferent; it was complicit. It had created a system where her safety, her children's safety, was secondary to its rigid rules and unyielding algorithms.

For a moment, she sat frozen, the weight of hopelessness pressing down on her like a physical force. But as the silence of the house wrapped around her, something else began to stir deep within—a quiet yet unrelenting resolve. If NEXT wasn't going to help her, she would have to find a way out herself, no matter what it took. There was a pause on the line, the faint clicking of a keyboard filling the silence as Valerie clutched the phone tightly, her hope slipping away with every passing second. When the agent finally spoke again, their voice remained devoid of empathy, as if this was just another mundane inquiry. "I'm afraid there's nothing in our policy that allows for termination based on the grounds you've mentioned," they said, their tone clinical, dismissive. "Our suggestion would be to work within the confines of your match agreement and perhaps consider seeking external counseling services to address any relationship challenges."

The words stung, hollow and impersonal, as if her fears were nothing more than a checkbox on a form they had no interest in addressing. Valerie sat in stunned silence for a moment, her mind reeling, before she abruptly hung up the phone. The weight of their indifference crashed over her, settling heavily on her chest. It wasn't just Derek she was fighting against—it was a system that had reduced her life to a transaction, a set of rules she was expected to obey without question. Her heart sank, the realization hitting her with brutal clarity. She had traded David away, believing it was a step toward something better, a chance to rebuild her life. Instead, she had walked straight into a nightmare. This wasn't a fresh start—it was a prison sentence, one with no appeal, no parole. She glanced down the dim hallway, where the faint outlines of her children's bedrooms loomed like silent witnesses to her failure. They were likely awake, huddled in their beds, their small bodies curled up against the cold fear that had permeated their home since Derek's arrival. She hated that they could sense her fear, that they were forced to share in her helplessness.

The following days blurred together in a haze of dread and mounting tension. Derek's behavior became more erratic, more unnerving with each passing moment. He began sharing bits of his past, dropping dark hints and chilling confessions as though they were badges of honor. "Got into plenty of fights growing up," he said one evening, his voice casual but his eyes glinting with something predatory. "Picked up a record for a while—nothing too serious, but enough to let people know not to mess with me." He chuckled, the sound low and humorless. "You'd be surprised what I'm capable of when I'm pushed."

Each revelation felt like a calculated move, designed to unsettle her, to remind her of the danger she was living with. He seemed to enjoy watching her reaction, the subtle tightening of her jaw, the way her eyes flickered with unease. The fear she tried so hard to suppress only seemed to feed him, embolden him. It was a game to him, one he was determined to win by breaking her completely. Valerie tried to put on a brave face, to shield her children from the growing storm, but Derek's shadow loomed too large, his presence too oppressive to ignore. Every glance he cast her way, every veiled threat disguised as a casual remark, chipped away at her resolve. The more he revealed about his past—the fights, the violence, the criminal record—the more trapped she felt. The walls of her home, once a sanctuary, now felt like they were closing in, suffocating her under the weight of his control. And worst of all, the system that had put him there refused to acknowledge her plight, leaving her to fend for herself in a battle she wasn't sure she could win.

Late one night, after Derek had finally stormed out into the cold darkness, Valerie sat alone at the kitchen table. The house was eerily quiet, the kind of silence that amplified every creak, every groan of the old floorboards. Her hands gripped the edge of the table as if holding on to something tangible could keep her from unraveling completely. The weight of her decisions, the suffocating presence of Derek, and the gnawing fear for her children pressed down on her like a crushing tide. The kitchen light cast long shadows across the room, a visual reminder of the darkness that now engulfed her life. She had believed, foolishly perhaps, that the NEXT system could be her escape—a way to rewrite her story and leave behind the monotony and dissatisfaction of her past. But sitting there now, her shoulders hunched and her breathing shallow, she realized the bitter irony of it all. The truth, cold and unyielding, stared her in the face: the system didn't care about her life, her safety, or her happiness. It had never been about helping people. NEXT cared only about control—control over its users, their choices, and their futures. It didn't matter what lives were destroyed in the process, as long as the numbers in its algorithm added up. Her phone buzzed, the harsh glow of the screen cutting through the dim kitchen. She hesitated before picking it up, her stomach twisting in anticipation of another cryptic message from Derek or perhaps another dismissive response from the support line. Instead, it was a notification from NEXT. She stared at the words on the screen, her lips curling into a bitter half-smile that bordered on a grimace.

"Your match with Derek is stable. Congratulations!"

For a moment, she thought she might laugh, the absurdity of it too much to bear. Stable. That was their word for the disaster her life had become. To NEXT, stability meant a lack of official complaints, a lack of disruptions that couldn't be ignored. It didn't matter if she was terrified in her own home, if her children tiptoed around a man who relished their fear. As far as the system was concerned, her new life was unfolding exactly as intended. She was just another data point, another box checked off in their glowing performance reports.

The anger burned through her despair, sharp and unrelenting. She wanted to throw the phone across the room, to scream at the faceless architects of this nightmare. But she knew it wouldn't change anything. NEXT didn't care about her rage, her tears, or her fear. It wouldn't care until she either conformed or disappeared. And maybe that was the key. As Valerie sat there, the faint sounds of the night filtering through the cracked window, a seed of an idea began to take root. If the system saw her as just another number, then perhaps she could become invisible to it. For the first time in weeks, she felt a glimmer of something other than dread. It wasn't hope, not yet, but it was close—a faint spark of defiance, a refusal to let the system and Derek decide the rest of her story. Her hands stopped trembling as she placed the phone back on the table. She didn't know how she would do it or what it would cost, but one thing was certain: she wasn't going to let NEXT or Derek have the final say. If they wanted her to play by their rules, she would find a way to break free. One way or another, she would reclaim her life.

But the fear that gripped Valerie was all too real. Derek was real—the unpredictable menace in her home, the shadow that loomed over her every moment. The threat he posed to her children wasn't some abstract worry; it was a living, breathing danger that weighed on her every decision. As she stared at the notification glowing mockingly on her phone, its sterile congratulation a cruel contrast to her turmoil, she knew that escaping this nightmare would be no easy feat. The system wasn't going to save her. The authorities wouldn't intervene, bound by bureaucracy and the ironclad contracts that NEXT had so cleverly engineered. And wishing, hoping, praying that Derek would leave on his own? That was a fantasy, a naive dream she couldn't afford to entertain. If anything, Derek's control over her was growing stronger with each passing day, tightening around her like a vise.

Her life, and more urgently, her children's lives, depended on her finding a way out. But as she sat there, frozen in the suffocating stillness of the kitchen, the weight of her reality pressed down on her like a heavy shroud. Every option felt impossible, every path fraught with danger. How could she run when Derek watched her every move? How could she keep her children safe when they were just as much prisoners in this twisted match as she was? For now, all she could feel was the crushing sense of entrapment. This wasn't just a nightmare; it was a prison of her own making, one she had willingly stepped into when she thought NEXT could offer her a better life. Every breath she took seemed harder than the last, as if the walls were closing in, suffocating her more each time she tried to inhale. But even in the darkest corners of her despair, a flicker of determination remained. It was faint, barely a spark, but it was there, buried beneath the fear and the guilt. She couldn't afford to let it die. For her children's sake, for her own survival, she would have to find a way to turn that spark into a fire. The nightmare might be tightening around her, but Valerie wasn't ready to let it consume her just yet.

CHAPTER FIVE

The rain drummed steadily on the roof of the small café where David sat, his hand gripping the paper cup of lukewarm coffee so tightly that his knuckles turned white. The muted chatter of other patrons faded into the background, drowned out by the rhythmic patter of rain and the weight of the conversation unfolding. Across from him sat a man who had introduced himself only as "Gray." Everything about Gray, from his nondescript clothing to the guarded way he scanned the room, exuded an air of caution. His expression was as unreadable as a locked safe, but his weathered face and sunken eyes betrayed the years of struggle and sacrifice he had endured.

David shifted uncomfortably in his seat, acutely aware of the risk he was taking. This meeting wasn't just dangerous; it was the first irreversible step into a rebellion he wasn't sure he was ready for. His mind raced as Gray's penetrating gaze seemed to strip away his resolve, leaving only raw nerves and doubt.

"You understand what you're asking for, right?" Gray's voice broke the tense silence, low and steady but tinged with a weight that made David's chest tighten. The man leaned in closer, his roughened hands resting on the worn tabletop. His tone carried a warning as cold as the rain outside.

"If you go through with this, there's no coming back. NEXT isn't some faceless corporation you can outsmart with clever moves. They have their own enforcement team, and let me tell you—they don't just scare people straight. They make examples."

David swallowed hard, his throat dry despite the humid air inside the café. He wanted to speak, to offer some reassurance that he had thought this through, but the words caught in his throat. The enormity of what he was planning settled on him like a weight he could no longer ignore. Breaking free from NEXT wasn't just a personal risk—it was a declaration of war against a system designed to crush dissent.

Gray's eyes narrowed as he studied David's reaction.

"This isn't a game, kid," he continued, his tone softening just enough to let the gravity of his words sink in. "People think they want freedom until they realize the cost. NEXT doesn't just ruin your life if they catch you. They erase you. And even if you're lucky enough to stay off their radar, you'll be living in the shadows, looking over your shoulder for the rest of your life."

David finally managed to steady his breathing, gripping the cup as if it were the only thing grounding him. "I don't have a choice," he said, his voice barely audible over the rain. He glanced down at the table, unable to meet Gray's piercing gaze. "I can't keep living like this. I won't."

Gray leaned back, folding his arms as he assessed David's resolve. For a moment, the older man said nothing, letting the tension build until it felt unbearable. Then he let out a long, weary sigh. "You remind me of someone I used to know," he said, his tone almost reflective. "Someone who thought they could outrun the system. Most of them don't make it, you know. But the ones who do... they're the ones willing to lose everything. Are you?"

David's jaw tightened as he looked up, meeting Gray's gaze head-on. His voice was firmer this time, though it still carried the tremor of a man walking a razor's edge. "I'm already losing everything. At least this way, I'll be choosing it."

For the first time, Gray's stoic mask cracked, just slightly. He nodded once, a flicker of something that might have been respect crossing his face. "Alright," he said, his voice low and deliberate. "But understand this: once we start, you're all in. No second thoughts, no backing out. If you hesitate, even for a second, they'll catch you. And trust me, you don't want to find out what happens then."

Gray didn't break eye contact as David reached for the folded piece of paper. The rain continued to hammer against the roof, the steady rhythm punctuating the heavy silence between them. The paper felt fragile in David's hand, yet it carried a weight that was almost unbearable. His eyes flicked down to it, but he didn't dare unfold it just yet.

"This is where you start," Gray said, his tone clipped and authoritative. "It's a safe house. Temporary. You'll stay there until arrangements are made to move you completely off the grid. But listen carefully." Gray leaned forward, his voice lowering to a grave whisper, every word measured and deliberate. "You have to disappear entirely. No contact with family, no phone, no internet—nothing. If they find even the smallest trace of you, they'll drag you back. And trust me, they don't just undo your escape; they'll make sure you regret ever trying."

David's grip on the paper tightened as Gray's words sank in. The enormity of what he was committing to pressed down on him like a crushing weight. Disappearing wasn't just leaving Linda or escaping NEXT—it was erasing himself from the life he'd known. It meant cutting off every connection, burning every bridge, even the hope of ever seeing his children again. He hesitated, his thoughts spiraling. Could he really do this? Could he abandon everything—everyone—just to claw his way out of the suffocating grip of the system? But then Linda's face flashed in his mind, her cold smile as she tightened the leash on his every move. He pictured the surveillance cameras she'd installed, the invasive way she monitored him, as if he were her possession rather than her partner. The thought of staying under her control was like a noose tightening around his neck.

He looked up at Gray, his jaw clenching as he forced himself to speak. "I'm ready," he said, his voice steady despite the tremor in his hands.

Gray studied him for a long moment, his sharp eyes scanning David's face as if searching for any crack in his resolve. When he finally nodded, it was slow and deliberate, an acknowledgment of David's decision rather than approval. He reached into his jacket and slid a small burner phone across the table.

"You'll get a message when it's time to move," Gray said, his tone as cold as the rain outside. "Until then, don't contact me. Don't call anyone. Don't do anything stupid to tip her off. You keep your head down, you follow every instruction to the letter, and maybe—just maybe—you'll pull this off."

David nodded, slipping the burner phone into his pocket alongside the folded paper. He wanted to ask Gray how many others had tried, how many had succeeded, but he couldn't bring himself to voice the question. Some things were better left unknown.

Gray pushed back his chair, the screech of metal legs against the floor cutting through the low hum of the café. "This is your only chance, David," he said, his tone a final warning. "Don't waste it."

David watched as Gray stood and walked out into the rain, disappearing into the murky gray of the evening. Left alone at the table, David stared down at the coffee he hadn't touched, his reflection rippling in the dark surface. The burner phone felt heavy in his pocket, a tangible reminder of the life he was about to leave behind.

He closed his eyes, exhaling slowly. He didn't know what waited for him on the other side of this escape, but one thing was certain: staying wasn't an option anymore. It never had been.

The next week felt like walking on a tightrope stretched over a canyon, every step fraught with the risk of a fatal plunge. David spent his days carefully assembling the bare essentials for his escape. It wasn't much—a modest stash of cash he'd painstakingly siphoned from the household budget, a change of clothes for when he needed to abandon everything, and a small notebook filled with addresses and names, each encoded in a way only he could decipher.

He concealed these items in an old toolbox in the garage, choosing it for its decrepit appearance. The box was a relic from a past life, layered with rust and stuffed with a tangle of worn tools and neglected odds and ends. He knew Linda's disdain for clutter; she'd never bother digging through something so unappealing. Still, each time he added to his cache, he felt a pang of anxiety, imagining her uncovering his hidden preparations.

But Linda wasn't blind. She noticed the subtle but telling changes in his demeanor—the way he avoided her more than usual, his perpetual preoccupation, and the rare but telling moments of defiance that flared in his otherwise compliant behavior. Her suspicions began to fester, feeding into her already heightened paranoia.

Her questioning grew relentless, a barrage of inquiries designed to box him in. "Where were you this morning?" she'd ask, her tone sharp enough to draw blood. "Who were you on the phone with? Why are you late?" She scrutinized every answer, every hesitation, her eyes narrowing like a predator sensing weakness.

David felt the walls of his life closing in, the air growing thinner with every passing day. He knew he was walking a dangerous line, balancing the urgency of his escape against the need to maintain the fragile facade of normalcy. Each interaction with Linda became a test of his resolve, a calculated exercise in deception.

She started watching him more closely, her gaze lingering whenever he left the room. Her questions became traps, laced with accusations she hoped would trip him up. David countered her as best as he could, his responses calm and measured, but he could feel her circling closer, tightening the net.

In those moments, the tightrope felt even narrower, the canyon beneath him deeper and darker. But he pressed on, knowing that every step, no matter how perilous, brought him closer to the edge of the abyss—and the freedom waiting on the other side.

One evening, as David stood in the kitchen washing dishes, the sound of the water splashing against the sink felt louder than usual, almost deafening in the tense silence that hung in the air. He could sense Linda behind him, the weight of her gaze pressing down on his back. He didn't need to turn around to know she was watching him closely, her arms crossed tightly over her chest, her stance rigid with suspicion.

"You've been acting strange," she said, her voice sharp, cutting through the quiet. "What are you up to?"

David continued scrubbing the plate in his hands, keeping his movements slow and deliberate. His mind raced, calculating the best response. "Nothing," he replied, his voice steady, though there was an edge to it. "Work's been stressful, that's all."

Linda's eyes narrowed, a silent accusation settling between them. She wasn't convinced. "Don't lie to me, David. I can tell when you're hiding something."

He forced himself to maintain eye contact, even as his stomach churned and a knot tightened in his chest. He could feel the pressure building in the room, the weight of her stare like a physical force pushing against him. He couldn't afford to slip up now—not with everything on the line. "I'm not hiding anything," he said evenly, his words calculated, designed to deflect her suspicion. "You're imagining things."

But Linda wasn't fooled. Her gaze didn't waver, and for a long moment, neither of them spoke. The silence felt suffocating, the tension between them thick enough to cut with a knife. Finally, Linda broke the quiet, her voice colder now, more deliberate. "I don't trust you, David."

The words stung, but David remained impassive, unwilling to show any crack in his composure. He couldn't let her see how much her words affected him. He couldn't let her see anything.

Over the following days, Linda's vigilance only grew. She became like a shadow, always present, always watching. She picked up his phone whenever he left it unattended, casually scrolling through his messages and emails, her eyes scanning for any sign of a lie, any indication that he was hiding something. David began to feel the weight of her surveillance in every room, every corner. It wasn't just her eyes following him anymore; it was the constant feeling of being watched, monitored, controlled.

Even his errands were no longer safe. Linda began to follow him, driving a few cars behind, her presence lurking in the background, like an ever-looming specter of suspicion. Each time David turned a corner or entered a store, he could almost feel her watching him, her eyes fixed on his every movement.

David's every step felt calculated, his actions scrutinized at every turn. The walls were closing in around him, and with every passing day, Linda's control tightened, becoming a noose around his neck. He couldn't breathe, couldn't think, couldn't even feel safe in his own home. And yet, despite the growing tension, he couldn't afford to make a mistake. Not now. Not when everything he had been planning was so close to breaking free.

The night before his planned escape, David sat alone in the dim light of the garage, the faint smell of oil and rust mixing in the air. He had told Linda he was fixing the lawnmower again, a task that seemed to take on an endless loop in their lives, always needing attention but never truly getting anywhere. As he stared down at the toolbox, buried beneath layers of old tools, the weight of what he was about to do settled on him. His mind cycled through the plan over and over, each detail etched into his memory with obsessive precision. The thought of leaving brought a mix of relief and dread. He would leave early in the morning, before Linda was awake, drive to a secluded drop-off point, and meet with Gray's contact. From there, the plan was to vanish—no trace, no connections. It would be like erasing his entire existence. His fingers brushed over the handle of the toolbox, the metal cold beneath his touch, and he allowed himself a brief moment of doubt. Was this the right choice? Was it worth it? But every time the thought of Linda's suffocating control entered his mind, the answer came quickly. Yes. He had to go.

The door to the garage creaked open, and David froze, his heart leaping into his throat. He turned slowly to see nothing but the dark outline of the doorway. He exhaled, his breath shaky. Just nerves. He closed the toolbox, securing it in place, then stood up to leave. As he made his way toward the door, his phone buzzed in his pocket, the unexpected vibration making him jump. He pulled it out and saw the message on the burner Gray had given him:

Be ready by 6 AM. No delays.

David's fingers tightened around the phone as his chest tightened in response. He could feel the tension in his muscles, the pulse of adrenaline beginning to surge through him. This was it. The moment he'd been working toward. His escape was imminent, the door to freedom now wide open. A surge of emotion flooded him—anger, fear, determination, all blending together. For the first time in a long while, he felt something other than the suffocating weight of Linda's control. The thought of finally walking away from her, from the life she'd forced upon him, made his heart race. He glanced one last time at the toolbox, the symbol of his escape, then slipped out of the garage, the door closing softly behind him. He couldn't afford to look back now. Tomorrow, at 6 AM, it would begin. His way out, his chance to start over, to disappear from the clutches of a life he could no longer bear.

David's stomach twisted in knots as he stood frozen in the doorway. The sight of Linda sitting on the couch, so calm yet so utterly menacing, sent a chill down his spine. Her fingers traced the edge of his phone like she was savoring the moment, her expression unreadable but her eyes sharp with fury. The phone in her hand was th one he thought he had hidden—his real phone, the one he had been so careful to keep from her, the one he had used to coordinate his escape. He didn't even have to look closely at the screen to know she had found the messages. Every detail of his plans was laid bare. The drop-off points. The burner phone. The meeting with Gray. Everything. His heart pounded in his chest, and for a moment, the room seemed to close in around him. Panic rose in his throat, but he forced himself to speak, his voice hoarse, betraying the fear running through him. "Linda, I can explain—"

She cut him off sharply, her voice rising with each word. "Explain? Explain what? That you've been planning to leave me? That you've been plotting behind my back, making arrangements to disappear like some kind of coward?" Her eyes narrowed, her lips curling into a sneer. "Do you think

I wouldn't find out? You think I wouldn't notice the way you've been pulling away from me? That I wouldn't sense it?"

David's mind raced, but no words came. He felt trapped, cornered. There was no escape now. She knew. And it was worse than he had imagined.

Linda stood up slowly, her gaze never leaving him. "You think you're so clever," she said, her tone dangerously calm. "You think I don't know what you're up to? But you've underestimated me, David. You've underestimated just how far I'm willing to go to keep you. To keep control."

David's hands clenched at his sides, the heat of anger mixing with the fear. But he didn't dare show it. Not yet. "Linda, this isn't about you. It's not about us. I need out. I can't live like this anymore."

She tilted her head slightly, a cruel smirk forming on her face. "So this is how you're going to end it? After everything? You think running away is going to solve your problems? You think you can just walk away from me without consequences?"

David's heart raced, and his palms began to sweat. "I don't have a choice. This… this is killing me, Linda. You're suffocating me. I can't breathe. I can't live like this anymore."

For a long moment, Linda didn't speak. She just stared at him, her eyes dark and calculating. Then, slowly, she placed the phone on the coffee table with deliberate care, as though she was weighing her options.

"I think you've made a huge mistake, David," she said finally, her voice cold, almost detached. "But if you want to leave, if you think you can just disappear, then go ahead. Try it. But I promise you, you won't make it far. I'll make sure of it."

David's chest tightened. He wanted to argue, to shout that he could escape, that he could be free, but he knew it would be pointless. He was already caught in her web. And now, more than ever, he realized just how far she would go to keep him—how much control she had over his life, how far-reaching the system's grip on him really was.

He took a slow step back, his mind spinning, trying to come up with a plan. But all the sudden fear and uncertainty clouded his thoughts. He was out of time. There was no escaping now.

David's stomach churned as Linda's words sank in. He had never seen her like this—so raw, so unhinged. Her anger was consuming her, twisting her into someone he barely recognized. She had always been controlling, but now she was something else entirely, a version of herself fueled by betrayal and fury.

"You're not getting it," David said, his voice shaking but firm. "I don't want to be a part of this system anymore. I don't want to be yours. I want to be free. This—this isn't what I signed up for. You're not who I thought you were."

Linda's eyes narrowed, her lips curling into a sneer. "You think you can walk away from me? From this life we've built? You think I haven't made sacrifices for you? For this... for us?" Her voice was rising again, the fury in her words now a near scream. "You think you're the only one who's trapped? You think I'm some monster for wanting control, for wanting things to work? I built this. You belong to me now, and you'll never get out. Not unless I say so."

David felt a tremor run through him, but he steadied himself, not allowing his fear to overtake him. "I don't belong to you," he said, his voice quiet but resolute. "I'm not your property. I'm a person, with my own life, my own choices. And I'm choosing to leave."

Linda took a step toward him, her eyes blazing. "You think you can leave without consequences?" Her voice was low, menacing. "The NEXT system won't let you go. And I won't let you go either. You're mine, David. You signed the contract. There's no getting out."

David felt the walls closing in. He had known, deep down, that leaving wouldn't be easy. But this... this was worse than he had imagined. Linda's grip on him, on his life, was suffocating, and her threats were becoming more real with every passing second.

He wanted to argue, to fight back, to find a way out. But as Linda's cold, calculating gaze met his, he realized that there was no negotiating with her. There was no reasoning with someone who believed that everything—every inch of him—was theirs by right.

"I'm leaving, Linda," David said again, his voice shaking, but determined. "I'm getting out of here, with or without your approval."

Linda's laughter was dark and hollow. "You think I'm just going to let you walk out that door? You think you're in control now?" She stepped closer, her presence looming over him like a storm cloud. "You're nothing. You'll always be nothing. And when NEXT comes for you, when they drag you back, you'll wish you had never crossed me."

David's chest tightened as he took a step back, his breath shallow. The weight of her words hit him like a physical blow. The fear, the dread—it all came crashing down on him. The next few hours, the next few days, were critical. He had to be quick. He had to disappear.

He didn't respond to her threats. Instead, he turned and walked toward the door, trying to keep his breathing steady. But as he reached for the handle, Linda's voice stopped him.

"I'm watching you," she said, her voice low and venomous. "And I'll make sure you regret this. I'll make sure you pay for leaving."

David hesitated, his hand still on the door. He didn't look back. He couldn't. He knew the moment he left, there would be no turning back. He was no longer just running from Linda. He was running from the system. From everything he had built. From everything he thought he knew about his life.

David's hands clenched into fists at his sides. The tension in the room grew thick, palpable. Every muscle in his body screamed at him to act, but the weight of Linda's gaze held him in place. The stakes had never been higher, and with Linda now fully aware of his intentions, any movement felt like a misstep. The window of opportunity was closing fast, and with each passing second, the chance to escape seemed more distant.

Linda's eyes never left him as she reached for her phone, her fingers smooth and deliberate. She dialed the number without hesitation, her voice cold as she spoke into the receiver. "I'd like to report a breach of contract," she said, her tone matter-of-fact, as if discussing a trivial inconvenience. Her gaze, however, was fixed on David— intensely, without a flicker of doubt or fear.

David's heart thudded in his chest. He didn't need to hear the other end of the conversation to know the gravity of the situation. The system she was involving wasn't just a faceless entity; it was a machine that could track him, control him, drag him back into its clutches. His every move would be monitored, his escape a futile attempt in a world where freedom was a fleeting illusion. He could feel the noose tightening, a relentless pressure pressing against his ribs.

Her eyes glinted with cold satisfaction, as if she knew the power her words held. She was no longer just Linda— the woman he had once known. She was an extension of the system, a tool for its enforcement, and her control over him was absolute.

David stood frozen, his mind scrambling for a way out, but all he could think about was the phone in her hand, the call she was making, the inevitable consequences. The realization was stark and brutal: there was no escaping this.

Linda ended the call, her expression unreadable as she placed the phone on the coffee table with deliberate care. The silence that followed was suffocating, and David's pulse raced in the quiet aftermath.

"David," she said, her voice low, almost too quiet, "you've crossed a line."

Her words lingered in the air, the weight of them pressing down on him. He wanted to speak, to plead, but no words would come. The finality of her actions—the phone call, the cold precision with which she handled the situation—made him realize that in this game, he was already lost.

"Do you think I don't know what you're trying to do?" she continued, her voice a sharp contrast to the silence that hung between them. "You can't run from this. You can't outrun the system. You can't outrun me."

David swallowed, the taste of defeat bitter in his throat. He wanted to argue, to fight back, but her words rang true. There was no escape. Not anymore.

CHAPTER SIX

Trevor leaned back in his chair, rubbing his temples as the reality of it all began to settle in. He had once been a part of something revolutionary, something he believed could fix broken lives. The NEXT system was supposed to be a fresh start, a way to take the pain out of failed relationships. It was never meant to become what it had turned into—a profit-driven machine that thrived on the suffering of others.

He glanced again at the reports scattered across his desk. The data painted a bleak picture. Domestic violence rates were up, mental health screenings showed a drastic rise in anxiety, depression, and trauma-related disorders. But worse than the statistics was the human cost—the countless lives shattered by a system that was supposed to be a lifeline, not a noose.

Trevor ran a hand through his hair, frustration mounting. Every corner of the NEXT system he had tried to navigate led to a dead end. He'd spoken to victims—people who had been paired with abusive partners or trapped in relationships they couldn't escape. Their testimonies, if they could be heard, could expose the whole system for what it was: a business designed to exploit human failure. But no one was listening.

The higher-ups? They weren't interested in listening. They were too entrenched in the system, too invested in its success, to care about the casualties along the way. As long as the numbers were good and the media still saw it as a solution to societal problems, the damage didn't matter. They refused to acknowledge the rising tide of suffering. To them, it was just collateral damage—unfortunate but necessary.

Trevor's fists clenched at his sides. He couldn't just let this slide. The truth needed to come out, no matter the cost. He had been careful, meticulous even, in documenting everything. Every file, every meeting, every interview with a victim had been logged. These reports were his weapon. If he could just get them into the right hands, everything could change.

His eyes shifted toward the locked drawer in his desk where he had hidden the most sensitive files. They were the last shred of hope, the irrefutable evidence that the NEXT system had spiraled out of control. He had to be careful though—he couldn't trust anyone inside the system anymore. They were all too compromised.

The buzz of his phone snapped him out of his thoughts. He glanced at the screen: an anonymous message.

"The walls are closing in. You're being watched. Be careful."

Trevor's stomach sank. He had been cautious, but this message confirmed his growing fear: the system had eyes everywhere. He wasn't just fighting against a corrupt institution. He was up against a machine that would do anything to protect itself, no matter the cost to those it was destroying.

"Shit," he muttered under his breath, standing up from his chair.

His next move was clear. He needed to get the evidence out—fast. But first, he would need to meet with someone he could trust. Someone outside the system. Someone who could help him get the truth into the public eye without it being buried by NEXT's corporate and governmental allies.

With his mind made up, Trevor grabbed the stack of files from his desk. Every document was a piece of the puzzle, a testament to the lives ruined in the name of a utopian idea that had long since turned into a nightmare.

It was time to expose NEXT for what it truly was. But Trevor knew the danger of doing so. The system would fight back. It always did. He just hoped he could get the truth out before they silenced him too.

Trevor leaned back in his chair, pinching the bridge of his nose in frustration. His eyes scanned the papers scattered across his desk—victims of the system, each one a broken person caught in the algorithm's web. The stories were eerily similar, each recounting the same cycle of pain: people weren't finding partners through NEXT. They were being trapped in a relentless loop, recycled from one damaging relationship to another, with no space to recover, no chance to heal. The system that was supposed to be a solution had only compounded the suffering. It wasn't just ineffective—it was cruel.

The weight of the evidence, the growing list of casualties, pressed heavily on his chest. Trevor's fingers trembled as he sifted through the papers, each name a reminder of the damage that had been done. He couldn't ignore it any longer. The system he had helped build, the one he had once believed in, had failed so many. It wasn't the answer to broken marriages—it was the cause of so much more hurt.

But Trevor wasn't ready to give up. He couldn't. Not now. He had seen too much, and the thought of remaining silent sickened him. The people whose lives had been ruined by NEXT deserved better, deserved justice. He wasn't sure who to trust anymore—everyone who had once been an ally now seemed distant, perhaps even complicit. But he knew one thing with absolute certainty: he had to get the truth out. He had to expose the system for what it really was. If he stayed silent, the harm would continue, and the next victims would be none the wiser.

Trevor opened a new folder on his computer, his eyes scanning the documents carefully. His finger hovered over one particular file—Data Leak Report—and a knot tightened in his stomach. He had been looking for something, anything, that could serve as the piece of the puzzle to bring everything crashing down. This was it. If he could confirm the contents, it would be the smoking gun he had been desperately searching for.

With a deep breath, he clicked to open the file, his heart pounding in his chest.

What he found inside was even more shocking than he could have imagined.

The report was a bombshell. The government had been suppressing reports of abuse, manipulation, and even violence within the NEXT system for years. The evidence was irrefutable. Emails, memos, and internal communications between government officials and NEXT executives painted a chilling picture. Any complaint or report that even hinted at threatening the image of the system had been buried, dismissed, and hidden from the public eye. What Trevor had suspected was now confirmed: the NEXT system wasn't just failing—it was actively covering up its failures.

The higher-ups, the very people who had orchestrated the system's creation, had put in place a cover-up so extensive, so far-reaching, that it was nearly impossible to imagine how it could ever be exposed. They had manipulated data, silenced whistleblowers, and doctored reports—all in an effort to maintain the façade that the system was working. And as the years went on, the truth had been buried deeper and deeper, with more lives destroyed in its wake.

Trevor sat back, staring at the screen in disbelief. The weight of the discovery settled heavily on his shoulders. If he released this information, there was no going back. It would shatter everything—the NEXT system, the government, the very fabric of the narrative they had spun. But he knew it had to be done. The truth needed to come to light, no matter the cost.

Trevor's mind raced as his eyes darted over the damning text and figures on the screen. It was all there—every shred of evidence he needed to tear the NEXT system apart. The proof of abuse, manipulation, and an institutional cover-up. He could almost hear the weight of those lives calling out to him from the documents. But as clarity settled in, so did the suffocating realization: these files were classified. Protected.

If the wrong people discovered he had accessed them, it would all be over. No warnings, no trial. His career—and likely his freedom—would vanish in an instant. Trevor could feel the walls of the room closing in, his breath catching in his throat.

His gaze lingered on the screen. The cursor blinked at him, a silent metronome ticking down the seconds he had to make a choice. Exposing this information wasn't just risky—it was suicidal. The people behind the NEXT system had the power to bury him, just as they had buried the truth for years. And yet, the thought of staying silent felt far worse. How many more lives would be destroyed if he turned his back now?

His hand trembled as he reached for the mouse. He started copying the files to an encrypted drive, his stomach twisting with every progress bar that ticked forward. He was careful, methodical, double-checking every step. He couldn't afford to make a mistake.

Trevor's fingers hovered over the keyboard as he drafted a message to his most trusted contact—a figure within the underground network known for exposing corruption. They had worked together before, but this was different. This wasn't just whistleblowing; this was war.

He typed, his hands shaking: "I have something. Big. Too big for me to handle alone. Need to meet. Secure location only. Lives depend on it."

As the final file transferred, the progress bar flashed complete, and Trevor slumped back into his chair. His mind replayed the faces of the people whose lives had been wrecked by NEXT—Valerie, with her haunted eyes and trembling voice as she described the abusive matches she'd endured. Jason, who had lost everything trying to escape the system's grasp, his frustration and hopelessness etched into every word he spoke. And the countless others whose names he didn't know but whose pain had been laid bare in the reports.

They had trusted him, even when trust was a scarce commodity in their shattered worlds. They had taken the risk to share their stories, believing that somehow, someone would listen, someone would care enough to fight for them. Trevor clenched his fists. They needed him now more than ever.

The files were all here. Evidence of the lies, the abuses, the deliberate cover-ups. Trevor stared at the screen, the cursor hovering over the "send" button. His heart raced, the enormity of the decision weighing on him like an anchor. He could almost feel the weight of their stories resting on his shoulders. This is it, he thought. The moment everything changes.

But then, a chilling thought stopped him cold. His stomach churned as the realization set in. The government and the powers behind NEXT wouldn't stand idly by while he dismantled their empire. They had covered their tracks for years, silenced whistleblowers, and crushed opposition. They had the resources, the influence, and the ruthlessness to erase him from existence if it came to that. If they found out he was behind the leak, they wouldn't hesitate to take him down.

Trevor swallowed hard, his throat dry. The room felt suffocatingly silent, save for the quiet hum of the computer. He couldn't afford to act recklessly. The stakes weren't just high—they were life and death. He leaned forward, rubbing his temples as he thought through his options. Sending the files is only step one, he reminded himself. I need a plan. A way to protect myself. A way to make sure the truth gets out, no matter what happens to me.

He minimized the screen and opened an encryption program, setting up a secondary failsafe. If they came for him, someone else had to have the files. He typed furiously, his fingers a blur over the keyboard, driven by the urgency of what he had to do. This isn't just for me. It's for them. For everyone else who deserved justice.

Trevor glanced at the clock. Every second felt like an eternity. He had to move quickly, but carefully. The truth was now in his hands—but he knew the fight was only beginning.

Trevor stared at the screen, watching as the "Files Sent" confirmation message appeared. The weight in his chest seemed to grow heavier, not lighter, despite the action he had just taken. His hand lingered on the mouse, trembling slightly, before he let it fall to his lap. It was done. There was no undoing it, no taking it back. The truth was no longer his to guard—it was out there now, in the hands of those who could expose the system for what it truly was.

He leaned back in his chair, exhaling a long, unsteady breath. The room felt eerily quiet, the hum of the computer now a constant reminder of what he had just unleashed. His mind raced through the possibilities, the fallout. The people at NEXT wouldn't let this slide. They would come for him. They would come hard and fast, and Trevor knew he wasn't ready for the storm that was about to hit.

But hesitation hadn't been an option. Not when lives were at stake. Not when the victims of the system had put their faith in him. He had made his choice, and there was no turning back now.

Trevor's gaze drifted to the window, where the faint glow of the city lights flickered against the dark night sky. Somewhere out there, someone was already receiving the files, reading through the damning evidence he had sent. The thought was both terrifying and oddly comforting. The truth is out there now. It's no longer just my burden to bear.

Still, the reality of what he had done settled over him like a weight. His life, his career, his safety—all of it was on the line. And yet, despite the fear clawing at the edges of his mind, Trevor felt a strange sense of calm. He had done what needed to be done. Whatever came next, he would face it.

Valerie tightened her grip on the phone, her fingers trembling as she scrolled through post after post. The glowing screen cast a dim light over her face, highlighting the lines of exhaustion etched into her features. The legal jargon was overwhelming—restraining orders, custody battles, clauses, statutes. None of it felt tangible, just an endless maze of options with no clear exit. She sighed heavily, setting the phone down for a moment to press her palms against her face, as if she could push away the hopelessness threatening to overtake her.

Derek's control over her life was absolute, leaving her isolated and powerless. She couldn't remember the last time she'd gone outside without his permission, let alone enjoyed a moment of peace. The way he watched her, always with suspicion, made her feel as if she were constantly walking a tightrope. One wrong step, and the consequences would fall not just on her but on her children too. The thought of their small, frightened faces fueled a fire inside her, even as her fear threatened to extinguish it.

Her youngest, Mia, had started sleeping with the light on, claiming she was afraid of the dark. Valerie knew better. It wasn't the darkness that scared her daughter; it was the monster they lived with. Ethan, her eldest, had stopped asking for help with his schoolwork, retreating into himself to avoid drawing any attention. The home, once a haven, had become a prison where silence was the only defense.

Valerie picked up her phone again, her determination renewed. There had to be an answer, some way to break free. The forum threads were filled with stories of women who had escaped similar situations—some triumphant, others warning of the dangers and sacrifices involved. She couldn't afford to let fear hold her back, not when her children's safety was on the line. They deserved better than this life of tiptoeing around their father's anger, their laughter replaced by fear.

She opened a new browser tab and typed in a search for local support groups. If nothing else, she needed guidance—someone who could tell her what steps to take. Her eyes scanned the results, heart racing as she found a hotline number for survivors of domestic abuse. The words "You're not alone" stared back at her from the screen.

Her thumb hovered over the call button. She hesitated, glancing toward the closed bedroom door. Derek was in the living room, the sound of the TV blaring as he barked at a sports commentator. Her fingers twitched. If he caught her making this call...

But the alternative was worse. Valerie exhaled slowly, then pressed the button. She brought the phone to her ear, every second of ringing feeling like a countdown to something inevitable. When a calm, reassuring voice answered, she felt her resolve harden.

Valerie left the office, her mind clouded with the lawyer's grim assessment. The words repeated in her head like a relentless echo *The NEXT contract is airtight*. Each step she took felt heavier than the last. Outside, the world carried on—people passed her by, cars honked in the distance—but it all felt muted, as though she had been pulled into a bubble where the only sound was the lawyer's voice reverberating within her.

By the time she reached her car, her hands trembled as she fumbled with the keys. Sitting inside, she gripped the steering wheel tightly, her knuckles white as she stared straight ahead. Tears welled up in her eyes but refused to fall. She clenched her jaw, willing herself to stay composed. Crying wouldn't solve anything, and neither would giving in to despair. If the system refused to help her, she had to find another way. Her resolve hardened as she started the car, the engine's hum grounding her thoughts. Valerie didn't know how she would do it, but she knew one thing with certainty: she couldn't let Derek's grip tighten any further. For her children, for herself, she had to find a way to break free.

She began secretly recording Derek's outbursts, her phone becoming both her shield and her lifeline. Each time his temper erupted, she would discreetly tap the record button, her hands trembling as she hid the device in her pocket or under a cushion. His words were sharp, laced with threats and venom, each one cutting deeper into her resolve but also fueling her determination to document the truth. She knew these recordings could be her only way out—her proof of the danger she and her children faced. Every moment felt like walking a tightrope. Derek wasn't a fool, and his controlling nature made him hyper aware of her every move. She became adept at masking her fear, keeping her face neutral and her voice steady, even as her heart pounded like a drum in her chest.

It wasn't long before he started to sense the change in her. His eyes, always watchful, seemed to bore into her with a new intensity, searching for cracks in her façade. One evening, as they sat at the dinner table, the atmosphere was suffocating. The children ate silently, their eyes fixed on their plates, while Valerie focused on keeping her breathing steady.

Derek suddenly stopped mid-bite, placing his fork down with deliberate care. His narrowed eyes locked onto her, his expression dark. "You've been acting strange lately," he said, his tone low but filled with suspicion.

Valerie's grip on her fork tightened, her pulse quickening as she fought to appear calm. "I don't know what you mean," she replied, forcing a lightness into her voice that she didn't feel. Her words came out steady, but inside, panic began to rise.

"You think I don't notice?" he said, his voice sharper now as he slammed his fork onto the table. The clatter echoed in the tense silence. "You're hiding something. I can feel it."

She swallowed hard, every instinct screaming at her to run, but she knew she couldn't show fear. That would only confirm his suspicions. "I'm just tired," she said carefully, keeping her tone soft and even. "It's been... a lot, adjusting to all of this."

His eyes narrowed further, scanning her face as if trying to read her thoughts. The tension stretched unbearably, the seconds ticking by like hours. She felt the weight of his scrutiny, the oppressive force of his anger barely contained.

Finally, he leaned back in his chair, his gaze still fixed on her. "Tired, huh?" he said, his voice dripping with disbelief. "You'd better not be lying to me, Valerie."

"I'm not," she said firmly, meeting his gaze despite the fear coursing through her. "I just need some time to adjust."

For a moment, she thought he might press further, but then he let out a grunt and turned his attention back to his plate. "Fine. But don't think I'm not watching you," he muttered, stabbing his fork into his food with unnecessary force.

Valerie exhaled silently, relief mingling with dread. She knew the reprieve was temporary. Derek's suspicions were growing, and it was only a matter of time before he uncovered her secret. But she couldn't stop now. She had to keep recording, keep gathering evidence. It was her only chance to escape his grip—and to protect her children.

Later that night, Valerie locked herself in the bathroom, the cold tile floor beneath her grounding her as she scrolled through the recordings on her phone. Each file held the weight of her desperation and courage. She tapped on one, listening to Derek's venomous words, his voice booming with threats and rage. As painful as it was to relive those moments, she felt a flicker of hope ignite in her chest. This was proof—undeniable evidence of the torment she and her children endured. If she could just get these files into the hands of someone who could help—a lawyer, an advocate, anyone—maybe she could finally find a way out of this nightmare.

But that fragile hope was fleeting. Deep down, she knew the danger wasn't just hypothetical. Derek's temper was a powder keg, and if he ever discovered what she was doing, the consequences could be devastating.

The next day, as Derek paced the living room, his voice rising in one of his familiar tirades, Valerie sat on the couch, her phone resting inconspicuously in her lap. She had become adept at timing her recordings, waiting for moments when his focus was elsewhere before subtly hitting the record button. But this time, her luck ran out.

Derek's eyes snapped toward her mid-sentence, narrowing as they locked onto the phone in her hand. His expression shifted instantly, suspicion hardening into fury. "What the hell are you doing?" he demanded, his voice cutting through the room like a blade.

Valerie's stomach twisted, her breath catching in her throat. She quickly fumbled with the phone, trying to lock the screen. "Nothing," she stammered, her voice trembling as she forced a weak smile. "I was just... checking something."

His lips curled into a sneer. "Don't lie to me," he hissed, his voice low and menacing. In two quick strides, he closed the distance between them and snatched the phone from her hands.

"Derek, wait—" she started, panic flooding her as he unlocked the screen with ease. Her heart pounded wildly as he scrolled through the recordings, his face darkening with every passing second.

"You've been spying on me?" he roared, his voice shaking with rage. "Recording me like I'm some kind of criminal?"

Valerie tried to explain, her words tumbling out in a rush. "I didn't have a choice! You've left me no—"

"Shut up!" he bellowed, cutting her off. His grip on the phone tightened, his knuckles white with anger. Before she could react, he hurled the device against the wall with all his strength. The phone shattered on impact, pieces scattering across the floor like shards of her dwindling hope.

Valerie flinched, tears welling in her eyes as she stared at the broken remains of her lifeline. "Derek, please," she whispered, her voice barely audible.

But he wasn't listening. His chest heaved with the effort of containing his fury, and his eyes bore into her with a chilling intensity. "You think you can betray me and get away with it?" he growled. "You don't know who you're dealing with."

As he stormed out of the room, slamming the door behind him, Valerie sank into the couch, her body trembling. Her phone was gone, her recordings destroyed. All her careful planning had been reduced to nothing in an instant. But as despair threatened to consume her, another emotion began to stir—resolve. Derek might have shattered her evidence, but he hadn't broken her spirit. She would find another way. She had to.

He turned to her, his face inches from hers, his breath hot and heavy as he glared down at her. "If you ever try something like that again," he said, his voice deadly calm, "you'll regret it."

Valerie's breath caught in her throat, her pulse pounding in her ears. Every word, every syllable, was a warning—a chilling promise of the punishment that would follow if she crossed him again. She wanted to say something, to defend herself, to explain that she was only trying to protect herself and her children. But the words caught in her throat. The terror of his gaze made it impossible to speak, and all she could do was nod, silently acknowledging the truth of his threat.

Derek's eyes never left hers as he slowly turned and stormed out of the room. The sound of his footsteps echoed down the hall, growing fainter as he retreated, leaving Valerie in the suffocating silence of the living room. Her heart was still racing, her body frozen in place. The weight of the moment settled over her like a thick fog, pressing in from all sides. She had thought that her recordings—the evidence she had worked so hard to gather—would be her ticket out of this nightmare. But now they were gone. Destroyed.

She sank into the couch, her hands shaking as she stared at the shattered remnants of her phone scattered across the floor. It was over. Her plan had failed, and Derek had made it abundantly clear that she would not be allowed to escape. She felt a wave of hopelessness wash over her, the walls closing in, suffocating her.

For a moment, it seemed like there was no way out. But then, something deep inside her stirred—a flicker of defiance, a spark of something she hadn't felt in a long time.

She wasn't done. She couldn't be. Not while her children were still trapped in this nightmare too.

The escape plan may have been in ruins, but Valerie knew this wasn't the end. She wouldn't give up. She couldn't afford to. If she had to fight with her bare hands, she would. For her children, for herself, she would keep fighting until she found a way out.

CHAPTER SEVEN

David stood in the dimly lit room, his heart pounding in his chest as he zipped up a small, inconspicuous bag. Each movement felt deliberate, calculated. Inside were the essentials: a change of clothes, cash, a burner phone, and a false identity that had been carefully arranged by the underground network. This was it—the final chance to escape the suffocating grip of the NEXT system, the last opportunity to break free from Linda's clutches before the contract locked him in for good.

His thoughts were a whirlwind of panic and determination. He had known from the beginning that the plan was risky, but now, with Linda breathing down his neck, the stakes had become even higher. Her discovery of his escape attempts had changed everything. She was watching him constantly, scrutinizing every word he spoke, every action he took. There was no longer any room for mistakes. One slip-up, and he would be trapped—not just in the system, but in a life with Linda that he couldn't endure. His mind flashed back to the conversations they'd had over the past few days, her increasing suspicion, her biting words. It had become a battle of wits—her calculated moves against his desperate attempts to remain one step ahead.

Every glance, every breath seemed loaded with potential danger. He had to stay calm, stay focused. His life depended on it. David glanced around the room one last time, ensuring that everything was in place. He could hear the faint sound of Linda moving about the house, but he couldn't afford to wait much longer. Time was running out. If she found out what he was doing—if she realized that he was planning to disappear—everything he had worked for would be lost. He took a deep breath, trying to steady the trembling in his hands, and slipped the bag over his shoulder. With one final glance at the room he had spent too many nights in, he moved toward the door. It creaked slightly as he opened it, and his breath caught in his throat.

Every moment now felt like it could be his last chance to get out. He had to be quick, and he had to be quiet. With a glance toward the hallway, he slipped into the shadows, hoping Linda wouldn't notice the subtle shift in the air. Each step felt heavier than the last, the weight of the consequences bearing down on him. If she caught him now. David shook the thought from his mind. He couldn't afford to think that way. He had to believe in the plan, in the chance that, just this once, it would all work out. As he neared the back door, he heard Linda's voice from down the hall—shouting, perhaps, or just moving about, unaware of the escape unfolding just a few steps away. David didn't wait to find out. He slipped outside and into the night, the door closing softly behind him.

Freedom was just ahead, but the hardest part was yet to come.

David sighed, his hand hovering over the burner phone. The small device seemed to hum in his palm, as if it too understood the gravity of the moment. His thumb hovered over the screen, then tapped out a quick message to the underground network. Ready for pick-up. Are you sure this will work?

The reply came almost instantly, as if the words were already waiting to be sent. It has to. The window is closing. We'll get you out tonight. Don't back out now.

The message was brief, but the urgency in it was undeniable. David stared at the screen, feeling a knot form in his stomach. His entire body was on edge, as if every muscle was prepared to spring into action at a moment's notice. He took a deep breath, trying to calm the rising anxiety that gnawed at him from the inside.

He had no choice now. The moment had passed. The decision had been made. There was no turning back. David had spent too many years waiting, too many years under the thumb of the NEXT system, and too many years watching his life slip through his fingers as he tried to break free. This was it. This was the final chance. He had spent years plotting this escape, piecing together the details, and now it was time to put it into motion. His mind flashed back to everything that had led him here. The suffocating weight of the system, the years of lies, the broken promises, and the manipulation. He had tried to outrun the system once before, tried to break free from Linda's control. But back then, he hadn't been ready. He had been weak, unsure. Now, though, he felt something shift inside of him. He had learned to survive. And now, for the first time, he was ready to fight for his freedom, no matter the cost.

David looked down at the burner phone again, rereading the message one last time. Don't back out now.

His thumb hovered over the screen, but there was no hesitation this time. He pressed the send button with finality, committing himself to the next step.

It wasn't just about escaping Linda anymore. It wasn't just about escaping NEXT. It was about reclaiming his life. Taking control of his future. He had to go through with it.

I'll be there in ten minutes.

The message was sent. His heart was racing now. The room, once still, seemed to vibrate with the intensity of the moment. There was no time to second-guess himself. He had spent too long waiting for this opportunity, and now it was finally here.

David took one last look around the small apartment. The place had once been a symbol of his independence, his attempt to build something on his own. But now, it felt like a prison—an illusion of freedom that had kept him locked in place.

The underground network was ready. The escape plan was in motion.

David grabbed the bag that was slung over his shoulder, adjusted it one last time, and moved toward the door. Each step was deliberate, each movement calculated. There was no more room for mistakes. His heart pounded as he crept toward the exit, every sound amplified in his ears.

He had come too far. He wasn't going to stop now.

David's pulse quickened as his gaze remained fixed on the peephole. Through it, he could see nothing but the darkened hallway outside his door. The figure standing just beyond the threshold was cloaked in shadow, but the shape was unmistakable.

It wasn't a neighbor. It wasn't a delivery.

His mind scrambled for answers, each possibility darker than the last. Could it be Linda, already suspicious? Had she figured it out? Was someone from NEXT aware of his plans, waiting to drag him back into the system?

The knock came again, this time louder, more insistent. The hairs on the back of his neck stood up. There was no mistaking it now—whoever was on the other side of that door was not here by accident.

David's breath came in shallow gasps. He stepped back from the door, his body tensing, every muscle ready to spring into action. He moved toward the corner of the room, where his bag was resting on the chair, his fingers brushing over the strap, reassuring himself that it was still there.

A third knock. Louder.

This wasn't just a coincidence. This was no random visitor.

He had seconds to decide. Seconds to act.

David's mind raced through the plan. If he opened the door and it was Linda, or someone sent by NEXT, there would be no escape. He'd be trapped, and any hope of breaking free would be dashed in an instant.

But if he didn't answer, the risk of alerting them to his departure was just as dangerous. His heart hammered in his chest. He knew he couldn't wait any longer. The network was expecting him. His chance to leave was slipping through his fingers.

With a sudden decision, David moved toward the window. His hand trembled as he pushed aside the curtain, scanning the street below. He could see the dim glow of streetlights, the movement of cars, the distant figures of pedestrians. No one seemed to be paying him any attention, but that didn't make him feel any safer.

The knock came again, more forceful this time.

David's fingers twitched at the door handle. His thoughts, once clear, were now clouded with the urgency of the moment. He knew his time was running out. The door was a risk either way. But the decision was made. He couldn't stay here any longer.

With one last glance at the window, David moved toward the door, his hand steady as he reached for the handle.

David's mind raced as he stood frozen in front of the door. The two men on the other side were professional—too professional. He could feel the weight of their presence, the unspoken command they had over the situation. His stomach churned with the cold realization that they were here to stop him. To drag him back into the life he was desperately trying to escape.

For a moment, he considered opening the door, surrendering himself to the inevitable. He had no illusions about how this would play out. They would take him, force him back into the system, back under Linda's control. There would be no negotiation, no second chance.

But David had always been a fighter. The feeling of being trapped had driven him to this point, to this moment of breaking free. He wasn't going to let it end here. His eyes darted to the back door, the one leading to the alley behind the building. It was his only option now. He couldn't make it out the front, not with them standing there. The back door was a risk, but it was his last chance.

David's hand tightened around the doorknob, his muscles tense. He could hear the agents' low voices on the other side, the soft shuffle of their shoes as they stood in place, waiting for him to make a move. They knew he was in there. They knew he was preparing something, and they weren't about to leave until they had him.

There was no more time for hesitation.

David turned away from the door, moving toward the back of the apartment. His heart pounded in his chest as he approached the door that led out into the dark alley. He couldn't hear anything over the deafening rush of blood in his ears. His thoughts were a blur, his body moving on pure instinct. The door creaked slightly as he opened it, and David froze, holding his breath. It wasn't loud, but in the silence of the apartment, it felt like an alarm bell. The agents could be on the other side of the door in seconds. He stepped into the alley, closing the door behind him as quietly as possible. He wasn't out of danger yet, but this was a small victory. He had to keep moving. Fast. David didn't stop to look back. The faint sound of footsteps echoed from inside the apartment, and he knew they would figure out soon enough that he was gone. The alley was narrow, lined with old trash bins and the occasional flickering streetlamp. He moved quickly, blending into the shadows, doing everything he could to avoid being seen.

Every corner he turned, every step he took, felt like it could be his last. But he kept going, the weight of the bag slung over his shoulder acting as a constant reminder of the life he was running from—and the life he was fighting for. David's breath came in shallow gasps as he hurried through the alley, the dim light from the street lamps offering only weak guidance. The air was thick with the scent of damp concrete and trash, and every step seemed to echo too loudly in the silence. He kept his eyes trained ahead, aware of how vulnerable he was out here, exposed to anyone who might be watching. He wasn't out of danger yet—he wasn't even close.

He could still hear the faintest echoes of movement from inside the apartment. The agents would figure it out soon, but they wouldn't know exactly where he was. He had to make it to the street—any street—with traffic, with people, with a chance to disappear.

His fingers tightened around the strap of his bag as he rounded a corner, his heart racing. His mind was a jumble of thoughts. He couldn't afford to stop or second-guess himself now. If he made it to the main street, he could blend into the crowd. He could vanish, at least for a while. But his escape had already been compromised. He could feel it—the heat of pursuit, the urgency in every step, every shallow breath. The city was too quiet, too still, and it made him feel exposed. David pushed forward, his movements growing more frantic with each passing second. The night felt colder now, colder than it had before. It wasn't just the drop in temperature. It was the weight of the choices he'd made, the risk he had taken. His body and mind were on high alert, every nerve screaming at him to stay ahead of whatever was coming next.

As he neared the intersection that led to a busier part of town, he heard the sound of a car door slamming shut. His blood ran cold.

David instinctively ducked behind a dumpster, pressing his back to the wall. His breath hitched in his throat, and his muscles tensed, anticipating the worst. From his position, he could see the faint shadow of a car passing by, headlights cutting through the darkness. He knew what that meant: they were out there, looking for him. The vehicle slowed as it neared his hiding spot, the engine purring like a predator on the hunt. His pulse quickened, and the weight of the bag seemed to grow heavier, more cumbersome. His fingers ached with the need to run, but he couldn't risk being seen just yet. The car passed without slowing, but the tension remained, thick in the air like a storm waiting to break. David waited a beat longer, ensuring the car hadn't doubled back, before he allowed himself to exhale.

It was time to move.

He crept out from his hiding place, slipping back into the alleyway as quietly as possible. His mind raced through the options in front of him—he had no plan now. He was improvising, trusting his instincts to guide him. He wasn't sure where the next safe place would be, but he couldn't waste another second here. His options were dwindling fast, and he could feel the walls closing in around him. David's fingers brushed the burner phone in his pocket. He had one more chance to make contact with the network. He'd need a car, an exit route, and—hopefully—somewhere to lay low for a while. They had promised to get him out. But as he fumbled for the phone, a low voice called out from behind him.

"David!"

He froze. His heart thudded in his chest. It was too close. There was no way to outrun them now. The agents had found him. He wasn't alone anymore.

CHAPTER EIGHT

Her phone lay on the bed beside her, the screen still lit from where she had been scrolling through legal advice earlier. But now, it felt like a useless tool—just another reminder of how trapped she was. She had exhausted every avenue she could think of, every potential escape route. The lawyer had been her last hope, but all she had walked away with was a cold dose of reality: without Derek's consent, there was no way out. The system was too rigid, too impenetrable.

Valerie's fingers hovered over the phone for a moment, as if seeking something, some spark of inspiration to break through her despair. The next message from the underground network was supposed to be her salvation, but she didn't even know how to ask for help anymore. She had been waiting for someone to tell her what to do, to lead her out of this hell. But no one was coming. No one could. She glanced toward the doorway, hearing the soft shuffle of Derek's footsteps approaching. She tensed, instinctively straightening up. The familiar feeling of dread washed over her, her heart beating faster as his presence grew nearer. Valerie had learned to stay small, to become invisible in her own home, a skill she'd honed over years of abuse. But today, the thought of remaining passive felt like a betrayal. Betrayal of herself, of her children.

Her eyes flicked to the clock. Just a few more hours, she told herself. Just a few more hours until Derek went to bed, until she could have a few minutes to think. It was always the same—when he was asleep, she could breathe. But the moment he woke, it was as if she was drowning again. She stood up, pacing the room with the restless energy of someone who had spent too long waiting for a sign that never came. As she passed the mirror, she caught a glimpse of herself—a woman who once stood tall, a woman who had dreams, a woman who hadn't been afraid to fight for what was right. Now, she was a shadow of that person, clinging to survival like a desperate animal trapped in a cage. She felt the tears begin to sting her eyes, but she pushed them back, determined to stay composed. She couldn't afford to let Derek see any weakness. He would pounce on it, like a predator sensing an opening. His temper had only grown worse with time, his control over her tightening like a noose.

Suddenly, there was a sharp knock on the door, jolting her from her thoughts. Valerie froze, the tension in her body spiking. She knew that knock. It was Derek, and it meant one of two things: either he wanted something from her, or he was angry—again. The door creaked open, and his voice followed.

"What are you doing in here?" Derek's tone was casual, but there was an underlying threat in the way he said it. He always had a way of making everything sound like a question with an edge.

"I was just resting," Valerie replied, keeping her voice steady despite the fear bubbling up inside her.

He stepped into the room, his gaze sweeping over her, the scrutiny making her skin crawl. "Resting? Or plotting?"

Valerie swallowed, forcing herself to stay calm. She knew that look, the one that preceded his violent outbursts. She needed to defuse this, but she also needed to keep the facade up just long enough to get through the day.

"I'm not plotting anything," she said, trying to sound as neutral as possible. "I'm just... tired."

Derek's eyes narrowed, and he took a step closer, his presence overwhelming. "You'd better not be planning anything behind my back. You know what happens when I find out you're lying."

She didn't respond. She couldn't. He didn't want her to explain herself—he wanted her to be afraid. And she was. She was terrified, every second of every day. But she had learned to mask it, learned to keep her emotions in check so he wouldn't see just how much he had broken her. For a moment, Derek just stood there, his gaze locked on hers, daring her to flinch, to show weakness. When she didn't, he grunted and turned, walking back toward the door. "Don't make me come back in here," he said, his voice low and menacing. "You're not going anywhere, Valerie. Not now, not ever."

As the door slammed shut behind him, Valerie collapsed back onto the bed, her breath coming in shaky gasps. She wanted to scream, to rage against the unfairness of it all, but instead, she pulled the covers over her head, hiding from the reality she couldn't escape.

Her phone buzzed again, a message from the underground network flashing across the screen. It was time. It was time to act.

Sitting in the quiet of her room, Valerie wiped away a tear, a fleeting moment of despair threatening to overtake her. The feeling of being trapped had become almost suffocating in recent weeks. Every part of her life had become a prison. Derek's presence in her home had turned everything sour, a constant reminder of her helplessness. His manipulations, threats, and demands were suffocating her, and now she had no idea how much longer she could keep up the charade for her children's sake. They needed her to be strong, but the cracks in her facade were deepening. She had tried to record Derek's abusive behavior, tried to find a way out through legal means, but every door she'd attempted to open had slammed shut in her face. It felt like the world was closing in on her, and each attempt to escape made her more aware of how powerless she truly was. She had no real support system, no allies she could trust to help her. She was bound by the NEXT system, shackled to Derek by an algorithm that didn't care about her happiness, her safety, or her future. The system that was supposed to regulate partnerships had instead become a mechanism of control, one that kept her under Derek's thumb in a cycle she couldn't break on her own. The weight of it all was almost unbearable, and yet, she had to keep going. She had to keep pretending that everything was fine for the sake of her children. But the mask was slipping. With every passing day, it felt harder to hide the truth of her situation. As she sat there, her phone buzzed suddenly, cutting through the oppressive silence. Startled, she looked down at the screen, her heart leaping into her throat when she saw the name.

Carla. Valerie hadn't heard from her in years. After everything that had happened, after her life had fallen apart under the pressure of the NEXT system, she'd lost touch with most of her old friends. But Carla—she was different. Valerie had always admired Carla for her strength and resourcefulness. And now, here was a message, from a person she never thought she'd hear from again.

Valerie hesitated, her thumb hovering over the message for a moment. What could this mean? Was this real? Could Carla actually help her? Could anyone?

Her pulse quickened as she opened the message. The words seemed to leap off the screen, each one adding a weight to the growing hope in her chest.

"I know what's been going on. I've been following your situation on the NEXT board. I can help you. I have connections to an underground network. If you're ready to disappear, I can make it happen. But you need to act fast."

Her breath caught in her throat as she read the message a second time, trying to comprehend what it meant. The underground network. It was everything she had hoped for, but feared was just a fantasy. The idea of escape had been drifting in her mind like a distant dream, one she could never quite reach. But now, here was an offer that seemed too good to be true—an actual way out.

Valerie's hands shook as she typed a reply, her fingers pressing against the screen with urgency. How? What do I need to do?

The reply came quickly, almost too quickly. Meet me at the old diner on West Fifth Street tonight at 10. Don't tell anyone. Just you and the kids. Leave your phone behind when you go. Trust me, Valerie, I can get you out of this.

The words settled over her like a sudden rush of cold air. Meet at the diner. Leave her phone behind. The instructions were simple, but the fear was overwhelming. Could she trust Carla? The idea of going to the diner, meeting with someone who had been out of her life for so long—it was risky. But then again, what did she have to lose? Staying with Derek? Being trapped in the system forever? That wasn't an option anymore. The thought of disappearing, of running away from everything she knew, felt terrifying. The fear of the unknown, of leaving behind the life she had built—even though it was falling apart—chilled her to the bone. But staying with Derek? That was no longer an option.

Valerie quickly typed her response: I'm in. I'll be there. I won't tell anyone.

As soon as she sent it, a wave of panic hit her. What if this was a trap? What if Carla wasn't really trying to help her, but leading her into something worse? There were so many unknowns, so many variables she couldn't control. And yet, as she sat there, staring at the screen, she realized there was no other choice. She couldn't stay. She couldn't keep living this life. The thought of getting her kids out of this situation, of finding them a better future, was the only thing that mattered now. She stood up, pacing the small room as she tried to calm herself. There was so much to do, so little time. First, she needed to get the kids ready. She couldn't risk them being awake when she made her move. She had to sneak them out in the dead of night, pretend everything was normal until the very last moment. It was the only way to protect them from Derek's rage, from the inevitable questions if he found out what she was doing. Her mind raced as she moved through the house. She had to act quickly, quietly. She couldn't afford any mistakes. Valerie grabbed a bag and stuffed a few essentials into it—clothes for her and the kids, a few personal items that she didn't want to leave behind. She thought of the house, the life she'd built, and realized just how much of it had been built on lies. Lies that Derek had told, lies that she had told herself to survive. She paused in front of the bedroom door, taking a deep breath before she opened it a crack. Derek was inside, his back to her as he sat on the bed, absorbed in the TV. The sound of the screen flickering was a dull background to the pounding of her heart. Valerie's pulse quickened, her throat tightening as she took a quiet step back. She couldn't afford to make a noise. She couldn't afford for Derek to wake up and find her slipping away.

For a moment, she considered going to him, confronting him, telling him she was leaving. But she knew that wasn't an option. It would only make things worse. So, she moved away, shutting the door quietly behind her, her heart pounding in her chest.

She grabbed the bag, heading toward the kids' room. This was it. Tonight, she would leave. Tonight, she would disappear. There was no turning back now.

Valerie stood over her children, her heart heavy with the weight of the decision she had just made. The room was quiet, save for the soft rhythm of their breathing, and in that moment, everything felt surreal. Her hands trembled as she gently touched their faces, brushing a lock of hair from their foreheads. They looked so peaceful, so innocent. How could she explain to them, one day, why she had to leave? Would they ever forgive her for taking them from the life they knew?

She had to believe they would. The world she had given them—one of fear, control, and manipulation—was no life at all. The NEXT system had already stolen so much from her, from all of them. It had taken their freedom, their security, and their peace of mind. But she could take it back. She could fight for their future, even if it meant breaking every bond she had built. Taking one last lingering look at her children, Valerie turned and crept back to the living room, where the bag she had packed sat by the door. It was light, but heavy with the weight of what it represented. A new life. Or at least the chance at one.

She grabbed her phone, glancing at Carla's message once more. "Be ready. Don't let Derek see you leave. Leave as soon as the kids are asleep. I'll be waiting."

She could feel the pressure mounting, the clock ticking down. Every minute that passed was another moment that Derek could walk in, see her preparing, and everything would be over. He would know. He would stop her. The consequences of failure felt suffocating.

Valerie moved to the door and opened it slowly, peering out into the darkened hallway. She hadn't heard Derek in a while, but she knew better than to think she was safe. The house felt eerie in the silence. She could almost hear her heart pounding in the stillness, as if the house itself was waiting for her to make her move.

Taking a deep breath, Valerie stepped into the hallway, her feet light but purposeful. She made her way to the back door, every sound amplified in her mind. A floorboard creaked beneath her feet, and she froze, holding her breath. But nothing followed. The house remained still, silent, unaware.

She reached the back door and carefully opened it, wincing at the soft scrape of the hinges. It was only a few steps to the alley, but each one felt like a lifetime. She stepped into the cold night air, the crispness of it biting at her skin, and closed the door behind her with a soft click.

The world felt suddenly so much bigger, so much more dangerous, but in that moment, Valerie realized that it was also her chance at freedom. She had made it past the first hurdle.

Now she just needed to keep moving, to keep running.

Valerie's pulse raced as she read Carla's message. There was no more time to think, no more time to plan. She had to move, now, before Derek realized something was wrong.

Her breath hitched in her chest as she heard his footsteps echoing through the house, growing louder. He was getting closer, and she had no idea where he was or what he was doing. But one thing was certain: she couldn't wait any longer.

With one last glance toward the back door, Valerie bolted toward the alley, her feet hitting the pavement harder than she had ever run before. The cool night air cut through her as she raced away from the house, her heart pounding in her ears. She had to get as far away from Derek as possible, away from the nightmare he represented.

Each step felt like a mile, but she couldn't stop now. Her phone buzzed again with another message from Carla: Stay hidden. Don't stop until you reach the diner.

Valerie didn't reply. She couldn't afford to. She couldn't risk the noise of her phone giving her away. The diner was still a good distance away, and she didn't have the luxury of a car or any way to travel quietly. She was on foot, and every shadow in the street made her feel exposed.

She took a deep breath, moving through the streets with purpose, slipping into the darkened corners, trying to keep her movements slow and steady. Her mind kept returning to her children, still at home, unaware of the chaos unfolding. She could only hope that this wasn't the last time she'd ever see them.

The thought made her stomach twist, but she pushed it down. She couldn't afford to break now. Not when she was this close.

As she neared a corner, she heard footsteps behind her, and her blood ran cold. Had Derek seen her leave? Had he somehow tracked her down?

Valerie ducked into an alleyway, holding her breath as she pressed herself against the cold, graffiti-covered wall. She waited, every muscle tense. The footsteps continued for a moment longer, but then they faded into the distance.

She waited a few more moments before taking a deep breath and stepping back into the street. She couldn't keep hiding forever. She had to keep moving.

When the diner finally came into view, Valerie's legs felt like lead, but relief also began to seep in. She was close. Just a few more steps, and she could finally see Carla. Finally be free.

But the cold feeling in her gut wouldn't go away. She had taken a chance tonight, and it felt like she had been running from the consequences for far too long. If Derek caught up with her, everything she'd worked for—everything she was fighting for—would crumble. She had to make it to the diner. She had to trust Carla.

She could only hope that her escape wasn't already too late.

CHAPTER NINE

David's heart hammered against his ribs, its frantic rhythm pulsing in his ears, as he darted into the shadowed alleyway. The night air was thick with the mingling scents of damp concrete and distant, decaying refuse. It pressed in on him, heavy with the tension of the chase. Every breath he took was jagged, shallow, a reminder that this escape was no longer just a plan—it was a race against time, and against those who were closing in on him. He had known, from the start, that slipping away wouldn't be easy, that the stakes were high. But now that the moment was upon him, the weight of it hit like a freight train, knocking the wind from his lungs. It was no longer just about evading the NEXT agents—it was a fight for survival.

They were out there, just beyond his reach, their presence palpable. He could feel the hairs on the back of his neck standing on end, like some primal instinct warning him of the danger. They were hunters, and he was the prey. Every sound, every creak of the alleyway, made him flinch, but there was no time to dwell on it. He had to move—had to stay ahead of them, even if only for a few more moments.

His eyes flicked briefly to the littered streets around him—the crumpled wrappers, the forgotten plastic bottles tumbling with the wind, the faint marks of neglect and decay that spoke of a world far removed from the polished, controlled existence of NEXT. But he didn't let the scene distract him. There was no room for distractions. His gaze remained fixed ahead, narrowed, focused. The path to the underground hideouts was etched into his mind, a series of turns and shadows he'd memorized in preparation for this. These hideouts weren't just safe houses; they were lifelines. The people who ran them were survivors—those who had outlasted the system. They were resourceful, dangerous in their own right, and above all, they understood the value of secrecy. It was a community built on trust, built on defiance of the very system that had nearly destroyed them. The NEXT agents had no idea how deeply entrenched their opposition had become, how many were still lurking in the shadows, biding their time. But David knew. And for the first time in a long while, that knowledge gave him a glimmer of hope. As his feet echoed off the wet pavement, he pushed deeper into the darkness, each step a reminder that the clock was ticking. The game had changed, and there was no turning back.

The rendezvous point was supposed to be a safe house on the outskirts of the city, a place where the oppressive weight of NEXT's control would finally lift, if only for a moment. If he could get there, David knew he would be among those who had managed to escape the all-consuming, suffocating grip of the system that had turned the world into a series of transactions and betrayals. These were the people who had fought to maintain their freedom, those who had slipped through NEXT's fingers and sought refuge in the shadows. But as David moved swiftly through the darkened streets, it wasn't just freedom he was chasing—it was something more, something deeper.

The underground network, the one he was about to join, was far more expansive than he had ever imagined. It wasn't just a handful of rogue individuals operating on the fringes of society. No, it was a movement, an organized effort that stretched across the country. Hundreds, maybe even thousands of people—men, women, children—had been trying to break free from the ironclad grip of NEXT. They had become the forgotten, the "disappeared," as the government conveniently labeled them, erasing their existence with the stroke of a bureaucratic pen. But David wasn't fooled. He knew better. He knew they were out there, scattered but not defeated. And as they moved through the cracks in the system, as they built their resistance in silence, they were growing stronger, gathering resources, and waiting for the right moment to strike. One day, David believed, they would rise up in unison. They would turn the tide against NEXT, and when that day came, it would be an unstoppable force. The streets blurred as David pushed on, his mind focused solely on the destination.

The safe house was within reach, but the closer he got, the more the weight of his journey settled on him. What if the network was already compromised? What if they were walking into a trap? It was a thought that gnawed at him, but he shoved it aside. There was no turning back now.

When he finally arrived, he found the safe house was nothing like he had imagined. There were no grand walls, no hidden underground bunkers. Instead, it was hidden in plain sight, nestled between two seemingly abandoned buildings on a street that was quiet—perhaps too quiet. The entrance was expertly concealed, a small, unassuming door that blended with the surrounding structures, its existence nearly imperceptible to the untrained eye. David approached cautiously, his heart in his throat. He knocked twice, a firm, deliberate knock, then paused for a beat. The seconds stretched, and just when doubt threatened to creep in, he knocked once more—faster this time, more urgent. The door creaked open, revealing a woman in her mid-thirties. Her brown hair was a tangled mess, and her eyes held a sharpness that cut straight through him. There was no hesitation in her stance—only a quiet readiness, a constant alertness to danger. She appraised him briefly, her gaze flicking over him as though assessing his trustworthiness in an instant. The door opened wider, and she stepped aside with little more than a curt nod.

"You're late," she said, her voice clipped, matter-of-fact, as if the concept of punctuality was something that still mattered in a world where everything had gone to hell. She didn't wait for him to offer an explanation. Instead, she motioned for him to enter quickly. He didn't hesitate. The door shut behind him with another soft creak, sealing them off from the outside world. The air inside was heavy, thick with the scent of old wood and stale air, but it was also filled with a quiet sense of purpose. They were safe—for now.

David stepped across the threshold into a dimly lit room, the kind of space that felt frozen in time. The air was thick with the scent of earth, as though the room itself had once been part of the natural world before being swallowed by the concrete jungle. There was also the faint, acrid aroma of stale coffee lingering in the corners, a reminder of long nights spent awake and on edge. The room was sparse, utilitarian, with mismatched furniture shoved together haphazardly—old chairs and tables, bookshelves crammed with tattered volumes, newspapers yellowing at the edges, and stacks of unopened mail. Each item seemed to have been placed with a specific, unspoken purpose, a piece of a puzzle no one was allowed to finish.

A few people lingered in the corners, their eyes on David, studying him with the quiet scrutiny of those who had learned long ago that trust was a commodity in short supply. There was no warmth in their gazes—only careful, calculating assessment. They were trying to figure him out, to gauge whether he was one of them, or if he might be a threat, another pawn to be discarded when he was no longer useful. A sense of wariness hung in the air, an unspoken tension that seemed to seep through the walls.

One of the chairs was occupied by an older man, hunched over a crossword puzzle, his focus entirely on the grid in front of him. His movements were slow, deliberate, as though he had given up on time itself. He didn't look up when David entered, as if he were accustomed to strangers passing through, too tired to acknowledge anything but his own quiet corner of the world.

The silence was thick, but not in the comforting way that solitude sometimes offered. It was a silence burdened by the constant threat of the NEXT enforcement agents, their presence like a shadow that could never be outrun. David could feel it pressing in on him—the knowledge that the moment they stepped outside, they were no longer safe, that their freedom was fragile, fleeting, and always under siege.

"This is David," the woman said, her voice softer now, almost a whisper. The hardness in her tone had faded, but there was no mistaking the weight of the words. "He's with us now."

Her introduction felt more like a formal declaration than an invitation. As though she were staking her claim, adding David to the ledger of those who had found refuge in this place.

Without waiting for any further acknowledgment, she led him through a narrow hallway, the walls lined with more of the same—books, clutter, and remnants of lives put on hold. The space felt small, cramped, the air still heavy with the tension of those who had learned to live in secret. At the end of the hall, they arrived at a small back room, where a handful of escapees sat together, their conversations muted, their words exchanged in quick, hushed tones. There was no cheering, no sense of camaraderie. It was as if they had long ago abandoned any hope of victory, knowing that survival was all that mattered now.

"You're among good company," the woman said, her voice a little softer now, but the warning still hung in her words. "But you should know, life here is just as precarious. NEXT's agents are always looking. They'll stop at nothing to find us."

Her eyes met David's, a flicker of something—determination or maybe resignation—passing between them. She wasn't offering him comfort, and she wasn't here to make him feel better about the choices he had made. She was simply laying the truth out for him, as brutal and unvarnished as it was. The stakes were high, and the risks were real. There were no guarantees, no assurances that he would wake up the next morning with the same freedom he had when he arrived. David nodded, acknowledging the gravity of her words, but didn't speak. He knew that survival wasn't a promise; it was a constant, shifting game of evasion, of being one step ahead of the ones who hunted them.

He took a seat next to a man who couldn't have been much older than thirty, though his face was marked by the weariness of someone who had aged decades in the span of a few short months. There was a haunted look in his eyes, the kind of exhaustion that didn't come from lack of sleep but from the toll of living constantly on edge, from never knowing when the next knock on the door would come, when the next chase would begin. The man glanced at David briefly, offering a small, tight-lipped smile—a gesture that seemed more out of habit than anything else. He didn't offer a handshake or any words of welcome. Instead, he simply stared at the floor for a long moment, as if he were trying to determine whether David belonged here, whether he would last long enough to matter.

In this world, David realized, time wasn't measured in hours or days. It was measured in moments—those fleeting instances when you realized you were still alive, when you realized you hadn't been found yet. But with each passing second, those moments became fewer and farther between.

The man studied David for a long moment, his eyes narrowing as if weighing the words he was about to speak. There was a hard, almost cynical edge to his gaze, as though he had long ago learned not to expect much from anyone, least of all newcomers who still held the luxury of hope.

"How long you been running?" he asked, his voice rough and raspy, like it hadn't been used much in recent days, or perhaps even years. It was a voice that came from the depths of experience—gritty, raw, and laced with the fatigue of someone who had lived a thousand lifetimes in a fraction of the time. The question hung in the air, heavy with meaning. This was more than small talk. It was an inquiry into survival, into the kind of life David had been forced to adopt.

"Not long enough," David muttered, his thoughts momentarily consumed by the echo of footsteps just beyond the walls, the threat of NEXT's agents constantly looming over him. His heart thudded in his chest, each beat a reminder of how close the danger was, how quickly things could go from bad to worse. "But I'm guessing you've been doing this for years," he added, his voice tinged with a weary respect, acknowledging the man's hardened exterior, his clear experience in evading the system.

The man's lips twitched, a hollow chuckle escaping him as he shook his head slowly. It wasn't a sound of humor—it was the bitter laugh of someone who had seen too much, had lost too much. "Longer than that," he said, his words weighted with years of struggle. "You're just starting to see what we've been dealing with. The NEXT system doesn't just take your freedom; it takes your future, your family, your life. All for the sake of control."

His voice dropped lower, his eyes shifting away from David as if to avoid the memories that were surely surfacing. He exhaled slowly, as though expelling the words from a place deep inside him that he'd buried for too long. "It's not just a job for those agents. They believe in it. That's what makes them dangerous."

David's stomach twisted at the man's words. They struck deeper than he had anticipated, the bluntness of them causing an ache in his chest. He had always known, on some level, that the system was corrupt—that it was designed to crush the people who dared to challenge it. But hearing it put into such harsh terms, spoken by someone who had lived it, made the weight of the threat feel so much more immediate, so much more real. He had thought of NEXT as an abstract force, something distant, impersonal. But now, sitting in this room with these people, the reality of their power, their ruthlessness, seemed almost suffocating.

David's thoughts raced. The faces of those who had gone missing—names he had heard, families who had been torn apart—flashed before his eyes. He had known, deep down, that these disappearances weren't just "government errors," as the media had claimed. But hearing it from the man sitting beside him, hearing the venom and the weariness in his voice, shattered whatever semblance of comfort he had clung to. These people—the ones sitting here, hiding in this dark, cramped room—weren't just victims. They weren't faceless statistics on a government report. They were survivors. Fighters. They had been up against a system that had taken everything from them, and yet here they were, still standing, still resisting.

David's stomach twisted again, but this time, it wasn't just fear—it was something else, something colder, sharper. A recognition that he wasn't just running from NEXT anymore. He was running towards something else. A fight. A cause.

He looked at the man beside him, his gaze steady now, more resolute. "I'm not backing down," he said, his voice low but clear. "Not now. Not ever."

The man nodded, his expression unreadable for a moment, before he finally met David's eyes again. "Good," he said, the word simple but loaded with meaning. "You'll need that. We all do."

The woman who had led David into the safe house returned to the room, her face set with the weight of urgency. In her hands, she carried a large, creased map, its edges worn from repeated use. She spread it out across the table, the faint rustling of paper cutting through the heavy silence as the others gathered around, their eyes immediately hardening with a shared sense of resolve. The room, already thick with tension, now seemed to pulse with the anticipation of something far more critical.

"We've got a problem," she said, her voice cutting through the quiet with the sharpness of a knife. "The NEXT enforcement agents are tightening their grip. They're not just looking for individuals anymore—they're looking for entire networks. There's a raid planned for tomorrow. We've got to move fast."

Her words hung in the air like a weight, the gravity of them settling over the group. David's heart clenched, the threat of a raid sending a shiver of dread down his spine. It wasn't just about escaping anymore. It was about survival—about making sure that all the work they had done, all the lives they had built and protected in the shadows, didn't come crumbling down in an instant.

David leaned in, his eyes scanning the map laid out before him. The network of safe houses, each one marked with a small symbol, formed an intricate web across the country, a lifeline for those who had managed to slip through the cracks of the system. There were routes, some obvious, others more hidden, that wound their way through the backroads, across rural landscapes, and into the cities, offering a glimmer of safety in a world designed to suffocate freedom. This was more than a few scattered locations—this was a massive underground resistance, a network that reached across state lines, that spanned miles of terrain. The sheer scope of it hit him like a wave, overwhelming and awe-inspiring. This wasn't just about him anymore. He was no longer a single target, a solitary figure trying to survive. This was bigger. This was a movement.

Hundreds of lives were at stake, each one interconnected by the fragile, tenuous threads of this network. People who had risked everything to escape NEXT's crushing control. People who had been waiting, fighting, struggling for a moment like this—the chance to push back, to take down the system that had stolen so much. David's mind raced, the possibilities unfolding in front of him. If they could expose the truth, if they could tear down the walls NEXT had so carefully built, maybe—just maybe—they could create a world where freedom meant something again. A world where people like him, like them, could walk in the light without fear of being erased.

David's hands gripped the edge of the table, his knuckles white. His voice, when he spoke, was low but filled with a strength he hadn't known he had. "Let's get ready," he said, the words spilling out with a determination that was more instinct than choice. His heart hammered in his chest, but his mind was clear. "We fight now, or we fight later. I say we fight now."

There was no hesitation in his words, no room for doubt. This wasn't the time for planning, for second-guessing. This was a call to action, to stand up or be crushed under the weight of NEXT's control. The woman who had led him into the room nodded, her face hardening as the resolve in her eyes sharpened. She met his gaze, her own voice steady as she echoed the same sentiment. "You're right. We don't have time to wait. Everyone, gear up. This is our chance."

The room seemed to come alive with motion as the others began to gather their things, preparing for the unknown. There were no grand speeches, no promises of victory. Just the sound of boots shuffling, weapons being checked, supplies being packed—each person moving with the practiced ease of someone who had done this before, who had been here too many times to count. They knew what was at stake. They knew that there was no turning back. And in that moment, in the midst of the chaos, there was an undeniable sense of unity that settled over the group.

David felt something stir within him, something he hadn't allowed himself to feel in months—hope. It wasn't much, not yet. It was fragile, almost imperceptible, like the first glimmer of light at dawn. But it was there. A flicker of something that burned brighter than the fear and doubt that had consumed him since he had broken free from NEXT's grip.

The rebellion was real. The fight was real.

And for the first time since everything had begun to unravel, David wasn't alone. There was a team behind him now, a group of people who had chosen to fight back, to reclaim their lives from a system that had stolen so much from them. He wasn't just running anymore. He wasn't just surviving. He was fighting—fighting for something bigger than himself, something that could change the world.

There was a war to fight, and for the first time, David didn't feel like he was running from it. He was charging straight into it.

CHAPTER TEN

The night air was thick with the scent of rain, the kind of moisture that clung to your skin and soaked into your bones. But Valerie barely noticed it as she hurried through the darkened streets, her mind too focused on the immediate danger ahead. Carla walked beside her, her presence a steadying force, while the kids stayed close behind, their small footsteps quick and light, as if they, too, could sense the fragility of the moment. The streetlamps, dim and flickering, barely illuminated their path, leaving them to navigate the shadows like ghosts, tiptoeing through a dream that could shatter at any second. Valerie's heart pounded in her chest, each beat a reminder of how close she had come to losing everything. She could still feel the lingering weight of Derek's presence, his hand closing in on her, just inches from grabbing her and dragging her back into the suffocating nightmare she'd fought so hard to escape. His control, the years of manipulation, the lies—everything she had fought against in her life had culminated in this moment. And tonight, it had reached a terrifying crescendo. The wall she had so carefully constructed around herself, her fragile sense of freedom, had almost come crashing down. It was too close. She had barely managed to slip through his grasp, her heart racing as she realized how easily she could have fallen back into that trap, that endless cycle of abuse.

They reached a familiar alleyway, one that led to a network of safe houses they'd used in the past. Valerie didn't hesitate, pulling Carla and the kids quickly into the shadows, her breath coming in sharp, shallow gasps. She could hear the faint hum of Derek's security vehicles in the distance, their flashing lights cutting through the mist, the harsh, cold glow reminding her of how quickly he could mobilize his resources. His reach was far, and he wasn't going to stop until he found her, until he dragged her back into his web.

But tonight? Tonight, they had slipped away. For now, at least. A small victory, fleeting but vital. They had escaped his immediate grasp, and that gave them just enough time to get further out of his reach.

Valerie slowed her pace, her hand gripping Carla's arm tightly. "We can't stop," she whispered, urgency in her voice, though there was a flicker of something else—a spark of hope. "We keep moving. We can't let him get any closer."

Carla nodded, her face a mask of determination, but even she couldn't hide the worry in her eyes. "We'll keep moving. But where are we going, Val? Where's safe?"

Valerie's gaze darted ahead, scanning the empty street, the darkened corners. "I know a place," she said, her voice low but steady. "It's not much, but it's far enough. We'll lay low, figure out our next move. We've got to stay ahead of him. We can't give him the chance to catch up."

As the group moved forward, Valerie's mind raced. The reality of what she had just escaped began to settle in, the weight of it pressing down on her chest. She wasn't free yet—not by a long shot. Derek would be relentless. But tonight, for the first time in years, she had a chance. She had broken free. And that was something she wasn't going to let go of. Not now. Not ever.

"I can't believe we made it," Carla breathed, her voice trembling with a mixture of relief and fear. She couldn't stop glancing over her shoulder, her eyes flicking to every shadow, as if the momentary calm could be shattered in an instant by someone leaping out from the darkness.

Valerie kept her eyes locked forward, her mind still reeling from the chaos of the night, from the close call with Derek. "We're not safe yet," she replied, the words slipping from her lips more out of reflex than any firm conviction. The truth was, she wasn't sure of anything anymore. The NEXT system was a behemoth—monstrous, far-reaching, and relentless. It didn't simply fade away when the lights went out. Derek's hold on her life, his entanglement with NEXT, went deeper than she could have ever imagined. No matter how far she ran, no matter how many walls she put between herself and him, she knew the system's claws were never far behind. The underground network had promised a safe house, a refuge where she and the kids could breathe without the oppressive weight of fear. A place where she wouldn't have to glance over her shoulder every five minutes, where they could finally start to heal. But Valerie wasn't naïve. She knew better than to trust in the illusion of safety. She could already feel the tension rising in her chest as the weight of what lay ahead settled on her shoulders. The safe house wasn't a sanctuary. It was a temporary shield, a thin layer of protection that could be pierced at any moment. The people who ran it weren't doing it out of charity—they were survivors, just like her. They didn't offer sanctuary without a price. Silence. Complete anonymity. That was the cost of escape.

Valerie glanced over at Carla, the woman who had been with her through thick and thin. "We can't let our guard down," she muttered. "This place, these people—they won't ask questions. But that doesn't mean we can forget who we're running from. Derek's not stupid. He'll come after us. He'll burn this place to the ground if it means finding me."

Carla's jaw tightened, and she nodded. There was an unspoken understanding between them, a shared resolve. They had to keep moving, keep hiding, keep fighting. And yet, the thought of her kids growing up under the constant shadow of fear made Valerie's stomach churn. She longed for peace, for a world where they could stop running, where she wouldn't have to whisper her every word, afraid that someone would overhear and bring the wrath of Derek—and NEXT—down on them. They turned a corner, and the narrow alley ahead began to open into the small enclave that was their destination. The lights were dim, casting long shadows over the narrow street, but there was a sense of calm here, a quiet that seemed to exhale into the night air. For a moment, Valerie allowed herself to breathe, though the relief felt hollow. She knew this wasn't the end of the road. It was just another stop on a long, treacherous journey.

"Let's go," Valerie said quietly, her voice firm as she guided Carla and the kids forward. The weight of the situation pressed heavily on her chest, but she couldn't afford to let it show. Not yet. Not with the kids still within arm's reach, not when the danger was still so close, lurking just beyond their vision, waiting to pounce. They arrived at the safe house after what felt like an eternity, each step through the maze of backstreets adding another layer of tension to Valerie's already frazzled nerves. The night seemed to stretch on forever as they weaved through alleyways and shadowed corners, always alert, always listening for the telltale hum of a distant engine or the flash of headlights that might signal Derek's pursuit. Each turn felt like it could be their last, each footstep a reminder that the illusion of safety was fleeting at best. When they reached the door, it opened silently, without so much as a word of greeting. It was the kind of quiet that felt more ominous than welcoming. The door shut behind them as soon as they stepped over the threshold, cutting them off from the chaos outside. For a moment, Valerie allowed herself to breathe, but even that felt like a betrayal of the vigilance she knew they couldn't afford to let go.

The house was small. Cramped. Barely big enough to hold them all, let alone offer comfort. The air was thick with the stale smell of long-forgotten meals and dust, the kind of scent that clung to everything, even the lungs. There were no warm, welcoming touches here—no pictures on the walls, no cozy furniture. Just the bare essentials: a few mismatched chairs, a threadbare couch, a table covered with old newspapers and what looked like a map of the city. It was a place built for one thing only: survival.

The living room was occupied by a few others, their faces gaunt with exhaustion but hardened by something else—something more resilient. Their eyes were watchful, alert, as if the house itself might betray them at any moment. The air was thick with tension, but it wasn't the oppressive kind that paralyzed you. No, this was the kind of tension that made you keep your head on a swivel, made you prepare for what was coming next even if you had no idea what that would be.

Valerie didn't have to look long to see that these weren't people who had come here seeking refuge from an oppressive government, or simply trying to hide from the world. These were survivors. They weren't here for comfort—they were here because they had nowhere else to go.

A woman with short-cropped hair and dark, watchful eyes rose from where she had been sitting, her movements deliberate, almost rehearsed. She didn't offer any kind of warm greeting. Her gaze flicked to the kids, pausing on them for a brief moment, before her sharp eyes returned to Valerie. There was no hesitation in her voice when she spoke.

"You made it. Good. We don't have much time," she said, her words clipped but not unkind. There was something in her voice that made it clear she wasn't just speaking out of urgency—she was speaking from experience. Whatever her story was, it had prepared her for moments like this. Moments when time was a luxury that couldn't be afforded.

Valerie didn't answer immediately. Her mind was still racing, spinning with the events of the past hours, the adrenaline that had kept her moving now slowly giving way to the crushing weight of reality. She could feel the heaviness in her chest, the shock of everything they'd just survived. But she knew better than to let it show. Not now. Not here. She squeezed Carla's arm tighter, grounding herself in the moment, in the reality that they were safe—

for now. But it didn't last long. Not with the way her mind kept drifting back to the faces of her children, their wide eyes full of fear, their hearts still carrying the weight of everything they had just escaped.

"We're here," Valerie said finally, her voice steady despite the chaos swirling within. "We're safe—at least for the night."

But even as she said the words, she knew they weren't entirely true. Safety was a fleeting thing now. All they had was time. Time before the next move. Time before Derek caught up. Time before the NEXT system closed in on them again. The momentary relief was nothing more than a pause in a much larger game.

Valerie's mind kept circling back to Derek. She couldn't shake the image of his face, twisted in rage, that moment when he had realized she was slipping away. The way his hand had tightened around her wrist, pulling her back just before she managed to escape. He had been so close—too close—and that thought gnawed at her insides. How could she have been so careless? How long would it take for him to figure out where she had gone, to tear apart every shadow until he found her? Once the NEXT system had its sights set on someone, there was no running. No hiding. Derek would stop at nothing to track her down, and when he did, she knew exactly what he would do to her. What he would do to her kids.

Her stomach tightened in knots as she recalled how Derek had used his influence to pull strings, how his connections had made it nearly impossible for anyone to escape his grasp. But that was before. Now, for the first time in years, she wasn't the one trapped. And yet, she knew it was only a matter of time before he made his move. The system wasn't something that let you just slip away unnoticed. It never forgot. And if Valerie had learned anything from her years in the grip of that system, it was that nothing ever truly disappeared. Not without consequences. The woman, whose name Valerie had yet to catch, didn't waste any time. She led them to a small room in the back of the house, its walls bare except for a few faded maps pinned on the walls. The air in the room was thick with the staleness of old memories and muted fear. She motioned for Valerie and the others to sit, and without a word, Valerie sank into the nearest chair, her legs suddenly feeling like they might give out beneath her. The exhaustion from the past few days—weeks, really—finally hit her, and she felt herself slump into the worn fabric. Carla followed suit, rubbing her arms and trying to shake the cold from her bones. Her body was tense, as if she, too, was still waiting for the other shoe to drop.

The kids, both of them still wide-eyed and unnervingly silent, huddled together on the ragged couch in the corner. They looked small, fragile even, in the dim light of the room. Valerie's heart ached as she looked at them, their faces a mirror of the confusion and fear she had seen too many times in her own reflection.

The woman, standing near the door, regarded them with a seriousness that was hard to ignore. "Listen," she began, her voice steady, though there was an edge to it, the kind that came from too many close calls and too much time spent running. "You're safe here. For now. But this isn't going to be easy. We don't have a lot of time, and the NEXT system doesn't forget. You can't contact anyone from your old life. No family, no friends. No one. Not unless you want to risk everything we've worked for."

Valerie's chest tightened at the woman's words. She could feel the weight of them settling in, pushing down on her already fragile sense of control. She had imagined a thousand scenarios of what life might be like after escaping Derek—freedom, security, a life where she could keep her kids safe—but she had never fully grasped the cost. The price of freedom wasn't just running; it was erasing every part of herself she had ever known. Her life, her history, the connections she had built—all of it had to be left behind. The people who loved her, the friends who had supported her, the family who had always known her—it all had to be erased. She swallowed hard, trying to push back the lump in her throat. The weight of the decision was suffocating, and she could feel it pressing down on her chest, threatening to crush her. But then, she looked over at the kids, curled together in their little corner, their innocent faces still holding onto some semblance of trust despite everything that had happened. They didn't know the full weight of what was at stake, but Valerie did. This wasn't about her anymore. It hadn't been for a long time. This was about keeping them safe. About protecting them from a system that would grind them to dust without a second thought.

"I understand," Valerie said, her voice sounding strange even to her own ears. She didn't feel like the woman she used to be, the woman who once had a life and a future she could plan for. That life had been shattered, and now there was only survival. "I'll do whatever it takes to keep them safe."

The woman nodded, her gaze softening for just a moment before hardening again. "Good. But remember, there's no going back. Not for any of us. If you want to make it out of this, you have to be willing to lose everything—because once you're in, there's no way out. Not without paying the price."

Valerie's mind raced. She knew the stakes. And as terrifying as it was, she also knew there was no other choice. There would be no turning back now. She had already made the decision when she took her first step away from Derek. The only question now was how much she was willing to sacrifice for her children's future.

The room seemed to close in around her as the woman's words settled in. Valerie wasn't just running anymore—she was part of a movement, a rebellion against a system that had already stolen too much from her. She glanced back at the kids, their faces pale and exhausted, eyes fluttering with the heavy weight of confusion and fear. They had no idea what lay ahead, no idea of the path she had just stepped onto. And she wasn't sure she did either. But there was no turning back.

"How do I destroy it?" Valerie asked, the words bitter on her tongue. "How do we even begin to fight something like NEXT?"

The woman took a long breath, her expression hardening once again as if she were steeling herself against the enormity of what had been asked. "You don't fight it directly. Not yet. That would be suicide." She motioned around the room, her hand sweeping over the sparse walls, the faces of the others who had gathered here in the same fight for survival. "You've got to strike at its core. At the foundation. We're not just fighting for survival, Valerie. We're fighting for the future of everyone who's been silenced by the system. We tear it down piece by piece. We expose it for what it really is."

Valerie felt the weight of the words, a cold realization creeping up her spine. She wasn't just escaping. She wasn't just running away from Derek or NEXT. She was now part of a war—one that had been fought in the shadows for far too long. And if she was going to be a part of this, she had to be willing to let go of everything. Her past. Her identity. The life she had tried so desperately to hold onto for her kids' sake. It all had to be erased if they were going to survive.

"I don't know if I'm ready for this," Valerie whispered, her voice breaking slightly. She wasn't sure if she was talking to the woman or to herself. But it didn't matter. She had already made the decision. The only choice she had now was to keep moving forward.

The woman gave her a hard look, her eyes unblinking, unwavering. "None of us are ready, Valerie. But the system doesn't wait for you to be ready. It doesn't care if you're prepared. It doesn't give you a choice. And if you're asking if you're strong enough to do this…" She paused, letting the silence stretch between them. "You will be. Because you have to be."

Valerie closed her eyes for a moment, the full weight of her new reality pressing down on her. This wasn't just about her. It was about every person, every family, every life that had been crushed by NEXT. The children, the elderly, the broken ones who couldn't run as fast or fight as hard. They were counting on people like her. People like them. This was bigger than her fear. Bigger than the pain of leaving her old life behind.

"I'm ready," she said, surprising herself with the steadiness of her voice. "I'll do whatever it takes."

The woman nodded once, her approval barely a flicker in her eyes. "Good. We start by disappearing completely. You've been running this whole time, Valerie, but now you'll have to become someone else. Someone new. And for that, you'll need to let go of everything. No more traces. No more ties. You'll erase yourself from the system completely. Start fresh, from the ground up."

Valerie nodded, feeling a strange sense of clarity settling over her. It was terrifying, but it was also the only way to protect her children. She wasn't just running from Derek anymore. She was running for them—fighting for them. The fear of what came next, of losing herself completely, was real. But it was a small price to pay for a chance at something better.

Her gaze shifted to the kids, still curled up on the couch. They were quiet now, their exhaustion winning over their curiosity. She wasn't sure when they would understand the gravity of their new life, or if they ever would. But for now, they were safe. For now, they were together. And that was all that mattered.

Valerie stood up, wiping her damp palms on her jeans, trying to steady her breathing. It wasn't easy, and it wasn't fair. But the future she had hoped for, the future her children deserved, was within reach. She wasn't about to let it slip away now.

"I'll do whatever it takes," Valerie said, her voice steady. It wasn't a vow. It was a promise.

The woman nodded, a glint of approval in her eyes. "Then let's get you settled in. You'll need to stay low for a while. But there's a bigger fight ahead. And we'll be ready when it comes."

As the woman left to check on the others, Valerie stood by the window, watching the dim light of the street lamps flicker outside. The world felt both impossibly large and suffocatingly small, and she wasn't sure which scared her more. But one thing was clear: there was no turning back now.

CHAPTER ELEVEN

Trevor Kline sat hunched over his desk, the dim light from his computer screen casting a harsh, unfeeling glow across his fatigued face. His eyes were bloodshot from hours of staring at the screen, his body slumped with exhaustion, but his mind remained wide awake, as sharp as ever. His fingers hovered over the keyboard, poised to act, but each second that passed felt like a weight pressing down on him—an invisible force gnawing at the edges of his concentration. The cursor on the screen blinked rhythmically, almost mocking him in its impatience, daring him to take the next step. He could feel it—the sheer gravity of the moment. Every action, every choice, could change everything. He had what he needed, all the pieces laid out in front of him: the documents, the encrypted communications, the damning evidence that could finally pull back the curtain on the NEXT system and reveal the truth, a truth so ugly that it threatened to tear apart everything it touched. But with every new piece of information he uncovered, the danger surrounding him only grew, creeping closer with every keystroke, every breath.

His phone buzzed sharply beside him, the sudden vibration breaking through the thick fog of his thoughts.

He glanced at it, his eyes narrowing at the unknown number flashing on the screen. For a moment, he hesitated, a flicker of doubt creeping into his gut. But it was fleeting. Trevor had long since stopped fearing phone calls, had long since shed the notion that anyone still cared enough to call him with good news. The world had moved past him, and he'd learned to accept that. He wiped his hand over his face, wiped away the exhaustion and the doubts, and answered the call with a sharp, professional edge. "Trevor Kline." His voice was a cool, practiced monotone, revealing nothing of the tension thrumming beneath his skin.

The voice on the other end was low, rough, as if it had been worn down by years of hardship and distrust— someone who'd seen too much to ever sound anything close to normal. It held an edge of warning, a chilling quality that sent an involuntary shiver through Trevor. "You think you've got it all figured out, Kline?" the voice rasped, its tone thick with a knowing bitterness. "You think you're the hero of this little story? You've just scratched the surface. You pull that thread, and everything will unravel. But don't expect anyone to be there to catch you when you fall."

The words hung in the air like smoke, thick and oppressive, wrapping around him until the space seemed to close in. Before Trevor could respond, the line went dead with an abrupt click, leaving him alone with the sound of his own heartbeat thumping in his ears. The silence that followed was deafening, more oppressive than the voice itself. He stared at the phone for what felt like an eternity, watching the screen flicker once before it fell silent. His mind raced, his thoughts spiraling. He should have been scared—he should have felt the cold grip of fear settle in. It was the kind of warning that could shatter any sense of security. But it didn't. Not for Trevor. Not anymore.

Instead, all he could think about was the file he'd painstakingly compiled—the evidence sitting there, waiting, ready to expose the truth. Irrefutable. Solid. Concrete. He had everything: the communications, the documents, the names—each piece like a jagged shard of glass, reflecting the horrors beneath the surface. The NEXT system was a monstrosity, a breeding ground for corruption and abuse. It wasn't just a few bad actors pulling strings from the shadows—it was the entire system, rotting from the inside out, so deeply embedded in every level of power that it had become a part of the fabric itself. It was an infection, a disease that festered unchecked. And Trevor knew that it wasn't enough to just expose it—something had to be done. People's lives had been destroyed, ruined, all because of a system that valued control over humanity, manipulation over compassion. Trevor had seen the evidence of that destruction firsthand, seen the way it tore people apart, piece by piece. He couldn't walk away now. Not when it had already gone this far.

The voice on the other end might have been trying to shake him, to make him doubt, but if anything, it only fueled his resolve. He had a choice now—either pull back, disappear into the shadows like so many others had, or push forward, knowing full well that there was no going back. Trevor wasn't sure if he was a hero, but in that moment, it didn't matter. What mattered was that the truth was out there, and it was his to expose, no matter what it cost him.

He stood, pacing restlessly around the cramped apartment that had become his sanctuary and his prison all at once. The walls, once a place of refuge, now felt suffocating, closing in on him with every step. His mind raced, constantly circling back to the same grim conclusion: the government was already watching him. He could feel their presence, like an unseen hand hovering just over his shoulder, tracking every movement, every breath. The weight of their attention hung heavily over him, more oppressive than the shadows that seemed to stretch out from every corner of the room. He had always known this day would come, but the reality of it was far more tangible, more suffocating, than he had ever imagined. His investigation—his search for the truth—had drawn unwanted eyes, and not the kind he had hoped for. No, these eyes were cold, calculating, intent on silencing him before he could get too far. He had been careful—too careful, maybe—but it was never enough. Now, the rumors were true. People had been tailing him, shadows moving in his peripheral vision at odd hours, always just out of reach. At first, it had been subtle, barely noticeable—a slight flicker of movement in the distance, the quick dart of a face before it disappeared into a crowd. But now, those threats were more than whispers. They had grown bolder, more daring, until he could practically feel their breath on the back of his neck.

But Trevor knew something that the government didn't. He couldn't stop. Not now. No matter how close they came, no matter how many eyes were trained on him, he wouldn't back down. He had already crossed a line, one that couldn't be uncrossed. The evidence was out there—pieces of the puzzle that needed to be put together. Lives were hanging in the balance, and he couldn't walk away from that.

As he paced, the rhythm of his footsteps was broken by a quiet, deliberate knock on the door. His body tensed instinctively, muscles going rigid at the sound. The knock wasn't hurried or nervous. It was controlled, measured—a signal that whoever was on the other side knew exactly what they were doing. Trevor froze, his breath catching for a split second. The knock came again, this time a little louder, more insistent. He approached the door, his heartbeat rising with every step. He didn't recognize the sound of the knock, the pattern unfamiliar. That, in itself, was enough to put him on edge. He moved toward the peephole, pressing his eye against the glass, scanning the hallway outside. The figure standing there was tall, the silhouette cast in shadows that seemed to deepen around them, hiding the details of their appearance. Trevor's heart skipped a beat. He couldn't place the person, but his gut told him this was no ordinary visitor. There was something about them—something important.

Without thinking, he reached for the door, cracking it open just a sliver. He peered out cautiously, eyes darting back and forth as he scanned the hallway. The figure didn't move at first, standing still in the dim light. Then, as if sensing his gaze, the person stepped forward slightly, enough for the light to catch their face. It was a woman. Her eyes were dark, the kind of tired, knowing look that spoke of long hours, long fights, and the weight of too many secrets. Her gaze held an edge of caution, but there was something else there too—something that made Trevor's instincts scream at him to listen. She wore a trench coat, its dark fabric rippling slightly in the draft that leaked through the cracks in the door. The coat was practical, but it looked worn, like it had seen better days—much like the woman herself. Her posture was stiff, guarded, but there was no denying the sense of urgency that radiated from her.

"Trevor Kline?" Her voice, though calm, carried an odd stillness that seemed out of place given the gravity of the situation. It was too measured, too deliberate.

"That's me," Trevor replied, his pulse quickening, a flicker of uncertainty cutting through the haze of his thoughts. His fingers hovered at the edge of the door, his grip tightening, as though the slightest move could set something into motion. "Who are you?"

The woman didn't answer right away. Instead, she glanced over her shoulder as if checking for someone or something, her eyes scanning the hallway outside before stepping forward, her silhouette darkening the entryway. "I'm someone who can help you," she said, her voice soft, but with an undercurrent of urgency that couldn't be ignored.

Trevor quickly shut the door behind her, his movements tense, the click of the lock punctuating the quiet of the room. For a moment, there was nothing but the thick silence hanging between them—charged, heavy, pregnant with the weight of unspoken things. The woman stood still, her gaze darting across the apartment, taking in the cluttered surroundings, the dim lighting, and the remnants of his frantic search. She seemed to weigh every detail, her eyes sharp, calculating, before she spoke again.

"I know what you're trying to do. I know what you've found," she said, her voice dropping a pitch, as if to match the gravity of her words.

Trevor's stomach tightened, his heart skipping. Hope surged within him, but it was quickly tempered by confusion. "How? Who are you? What's going on?" The words came out sharper than he intended, a mixture of demand and disbelief.

The woman paused, her eyes flicking briefly to the door as if considering whether to speak more freely. After a beat, she exhaled slowly, almost resigned. "My name is Kara," she said, her voice carrying a weight of experience that seemed to age her words. "And I've been where you are. I've been investigating NEXT for years, gathering evidence of the corruption that runs through it like poison in a body. But there's more than just the surface-level stuff you've found." She shifted slightly, her stance defensive but purposeful. "There's something deeper."

Trevor felt a surge of hope, but it was quickly dampened by a rising tide of unease. "What do you mean, deeper?" he asked, his voice a little too raw, too desperate for clarity.

Kara's gaze flicked to the window, her eyes narrowing as she scrutinized the street outside, scanning for any movement, any sign of unwanted attention. Satisfied, she leaned in, lowering her voice until it was barely a whisper. "You're playing with fire, Trevor. You're getting close to something they don't want exposed."

Her words hit him hard, like a slap across the face. They carried a weight, a certainty that sent a shiver down his spine. The implications of what she was saying sank in, but he couldn't quite grasp the full scope. "What do you mean by 'deeper'?" he repeated, his voice thick with both fear and curiosity.

Kara's eyes darted once more toward the window, ensuring they were still alone, before she leaned even closer, her lips nearly touching his ear. "The NEXT system isn't just a government tool for control," she whispered, her voice laced with the bitterness of someone who had seen the rot firsthand. "It's a business. A business with a stake in people's lives. They're not just controlling relationships or manipulating people's behaviors. They're making billions off of it, and they'll stop at nothing to protect that."

Trevor's body went cold. The room seemed to shrink as her words took root in his mind, growing like a poisonous vine, choking out everything else. A business? Billions? The scale of it all suddenly felt overwhelming, suffocating. He had known the system was corrupt, but this—this was something else entirely.

"But... how do you know this?" Trevor's voice faltered, disbelief creeping in. "Why haven't you exposed it yourself?"

Kara's eyes darkened, her face falling into a mask of quiet resignation. She lowered her gaze, her lips pressing into a thin line before she answered, the words heavy with the weight of unspoken fears. "Because it's dangerous. There are people inside the system who don't just control it—they've weaponized it. And if you blow the lid off it now, Trevor, you might not just lose your career." She paused, her gaze lifting to meet his, her eyes cold with the weight of what she was saying. "You might lose your life."

The weight of Kara's warning hung heavily between them, like a thick fog that refused to dissipate. Trevor could feel the gravity of the situation, the implications of what she had said, but something within him hardened—something deep and unshakable. He wasn't going to back down. He couldn't. This wasn't just about him anymore. It was about everything that had been wronged, about the lives that had been crushed under the weight of a system so insidious that no one even realized it was happening. His pulse quickened, and he felt the fire of conviction rise in him, pushing back against the mounting fear.

This was bigger than his job. Bigger than the threats. Bigger than the long nights he had spent, alone, digging through files and chasing shadows. This was about exposing the truth, no matter the cost. He clenched his fists, the muscles in his arms tightening with resolve. "I'm not backing off, Kara," he said, his voice steady, cold with determination. "I'm not just going to sit by while they keep ruining lives."

Kara studied him with an unreadable expression, her eyes narrowing just slightly as if trying to gauge the depth of his resolve. Then, a flicker of something shifted in her eyes—a momentary glimmer of respect, though it was hard to tell if it was for his stubbornness or his foolishness. She spoke again, her voice lower now, tinged with something heavier, something quieter. "I get it," she said. "You think you're the one who's going to bring it all down. But you're not alone in this. I've got someone who can help you."

Trevor's brow furrowed, a mix of curiosity and suspicion crossing his face. "Who?" The question hung in the air between them, the room too small for the weight of it.

Kara didn't answer right away. Instead, she reached beneath her coat, and with a swift motion, pulled out a thick folder. She slid it across the table toward him with an unsettling calmness. The weight of it, thick with papers, felt ominous in his hands. It was almost as if the folder itself carried the weight of everything he was about to uncover. Trevor hesitated before reaching for it, his fingers brushing against the cold surface, his mind racing.

"This is a whistleblower," Kara said, her voice low but firm. "Someone inside the NEXT enforcement agency who has the details you need to expose everything. But you need to meet them in person. They're risking their life for this."

Trevor paused, the folder inches from his hand, a flood of questions bombarding his mind. A whistleblower? Someone inside NEXT? It sounded too easy, too perfect. He stared at the folder for a long moment, his mind racing as he considered the risks. The gravity of Kara's words settled deeper with each passing second. Could he trust this? Could he trust her?

"How do I know this isn't a trap?" he asked, his voice rough with suspicion. His instincts screamed at him to be cautious. Nothing in this world was ever as simple as it seemed. He had learned that lesson the hard way.

Kara's eyes locked onto his, and there was a moment of silence between them—long enough for him to feel the full weight of her bluntness. "You don't," she said, her tone blunt and unapologetic. "But if you want to take down the system, this is your only shot."

Her words stung. It was the kind of answer he had expected, the kind of reality check that hit too close to home. But something in him recognized the truth of it. If he was going to follow this through, if he was going to do this, there was no room for hesitation. The trap could be real, but so could the opportunity. Either way, he knew one thing: there was no going back now.

Trevor's eyes remained fixed on the folder, the weight of it sinking into his chest like a stone. Every part of him screamed that this could be his moment—the moment that would unravel the truth, expose the rot at the heart of the NEXT system. But with every revelation, with each step he took, the stakes seemed to rise higher, like a tower of cards balanced precariously on the edge of collapse. The danger was tangible now, thick in the air, surrounding him with the kind of quiet urgency that only those who had been in too deep could truly understand.

One wrong move. One slip. And it would all come crashing down in a burst of chaos, dragging everything with it. Trevor knew that better than anyone. He'd been through too much, seen too many lives torn apart by systems that only cared for power and control, not justice or truth. The thought of losing everything, of failing now when he was so close, almost paralyzed him. But despite the gnawing fear that clawed at the edges of his mind, Trevor couldn't turn back. He couldn't back down.

"Where do I meet them?" His voice was steady, even though his insides were anything but. The words were out before he could second-guess them, and the hesitation that had been gnawing at him was drowned in the necessity of the moment.

Kara's gaze locked with his, and for the first time, there was no wall between them, no calculated distance. She saw him—saw the determination, the unease, the weight of what he was about to commit to. Her expression shifted, a flicker of something passing through her eyes—a mix of warning and the faintest spark of encouragement. "I'll send you the details," she said quietly, her tone far less certain now. "You're not in this alone, Trevor. But remember—there's no turning back once you make contact."

Her words cut through the haze of fear and adrenaline in his mind. There was no turning back. The truth was no longer a choice; it was a necessity. But as the last of her words echoed in his mind, he couldn't shake the feeling that this was the moment when everything changed. It wasn't just about exposing the truth anymore. It was about survival.

Trevor gave a brief nod, though it felt more like a reflex than a decision. His mind raced through the possibilities—the risks, the unknowns, the consequences. But deep down, he knew what had to be done. The next steps were no longer just his to decide. They were a part of something bigger than him, something that had been set in motion long before he ever stumbled upon the evidence. He had no idea what awaited him, but he knew that if he didn't take this chance, he would be complicit in the system that had destroyed so many lives.

When Kara left, the door clicking shut behind her, Trevor was left in the stillness of the room. The silence was deafening, a stark contrast to the chaos that was about to unfold. He sat back down at his desk, the folder resting in front of him like a heavy promise. He didn't move for a long moment, his hands clasped together tightly, his mind racing. Outside the window, the city continued on—unaware, oblivious to the storm that was about to hit.

Trevor had no answers. He had no way of knowing what the future held. But one thing was certain: whatever came next, he was ready. He would tear down the NEXT system. He would expose it. And in doing so, he would make sure that no one else would suffer the way so many had before him. Trevor Kline was going to make sure of it.

Trevor's grip tightened on the steering wheel as he made his way through the winding, dimly lit streets. His heart still thudded in his chest from the meeting with Kara, the weight of the folder heavy on the passenger seat beside him. His mind raced with the implications of what he was about to do—the meeting, the whistleblower, the evidence that could unravel everything. It was all so close, so within reach.

But as he took a sharp turn onto a quieter, less-traveled road, he felt a sudden shift in the air—a sense of something going wrong. The hairs on the back of his neck stood up, his instincts screaming at him to be alert. He glanced in the rearview mirror. The headlights of a black SUV were far too close, a little too steady behind him. The kind of close that made his pulse spike with unease.

"Just paranoid," he muttered under his breath, trying to shake off the feeling. It was late, the roads were empty, and paranoia was a side effect of the risks he was taking. He'd been followed before—he was used to it by now.

But the SUV didn't back off.

Trevor's hand hovered over the gearshift as he accelerated slightly, hoping to shake whatever shadow was tailing him. But the SUV matched his speed effortlessly. He could feel the tension building in the air, thick and suffocating. There was no doubt now—it was deliberate.

His eyes darted to the side mirrors again. The black SUV swerved slightly, speeding up to match his lane.

A flash of realization hit him like a punch to the gut. They know.

He cursed under his breath, his mind scrambling. He could already hear Kara's warning in his head, telling him that this was no longer just about a career or exposing a system—it was about survival. Trevor wasn't just dealing with a corrupt organization anymore. They'd been watching him for longer than he realized, waiting for him to make a mistake.

Without thinking, Trevor swerved the car to the left, aiming to lose the tail by cutting through an alleyway. But as he yanked the wheel, a sharp, metallic screech of tires rang out from behind him. The SUV was right there, its front bumper slamming into his rear fender with a bone-jarring impact. The car lurched, fishtailing dangerously as Trevor struggled to regain control. He fought to keep his car on the road, but the impact was too strong. The black SUV pushed him again, shoving him off course. His vision blurred as the streetlights streaked past, the sound of screeching tires and crumpling metal filling his ears.

Not like this, Trevor thought, his stomach flipping. I can't go out like this.

But the SUV wasn't letting up. Another hit. His car slid further off the road, tires losing traction on the wet pavement. Panic surged through him. This wasn't just a warning anymore. This was an attempt to end him. In a split second, Trevor jerked the wheel hard to the right, his car veering wildly onto the shoulder of the road, but the SUV followed, keeping pace. A final, crushing hit sent his car careening off the edge of the road, and before he could react, the car plunged into the dirt and brush. The world spun. Trevor's head slammed against the window as the car flipped, the crunch of metal and glass ringing in his ears like an explosion. His vision blurred, pain shooting through his chest as the car finally came to a stop, on its side, silent except for the faint hiss of the engine sputtering out.

For a moment, there was nothing but darkness.

CHAPTER TWELVE

Valerie stood motionless in the dimly lit room of the safe house, her senses heightened as the heavy silence surrounded her. The faint hum of the old refrigerator in the corner was the only sound, a sharp contrast to the chaos that had led her here. Her fingers, initially trembling with anxiety, slowly steadied as she wiped them against the worn denim of her jeans, feeling the coarse fabric rub against her skin. The action was reflexive, a way to ground herself, to remind herself that she still had control over her own body, even if the situation around her seemed to spiral out of control. The cold metal of the revolver pressed firmly against the small of her back, its weight both reassuring and ominous. It was tucked securely beneath her jacket, hidden from view, but Valerie could feel it there—its presence a constant reminder of the power she now held. She had never imagined herself in a position like this, never thought that she'd be the one holding the power, the one calling the shots. In a world that had often seemed to dictate the terms of her existence, it was almost surreal to think that today, for the first time, she was the one who had a say in how things would unfold. She had been the one controlled for so long, her life ruled by fear and manipulation. But now, everything had changed.

Across the room, Carla, her ally in this underground rebellion, was busy pacing back and forth, muttering to herself as she reviewed the final details of the plan. Carla was a seasoned strategist, always calculating, always ten steps ahead. She had been the one to suggest the trap—luring Derek into a confrontation he never saw coming, baiting him into a position where he would have no choice but to face the consequences of his actions. At first, Valerie had hesitated, unsure if they were ready for this, unsure if she was ready. But now, as the seconds ticked by, a growing sense of clarity began to settle within her. She had been living in the shadow of Derek's control for far too long, and this was her chance to reclaim her life, to finally break free from the grip he had on her.

It felt like the kind of plan a desperate woman might concoct, one fueled by years of humiliation and fear, a plan born out of necessity rather than choice. But Valerie wasn't desperate anymore. She had shed the weight of desperation long ago, had accepted that her fight for freedom wasn't just about escaping Derek's reach—it was about confronting him head-on, showing him that his power over her was an illusion. She had made her peace with the fact that she no longer needed his approval, no longer needed to cower in his presence. The moment she had taken control of her own destiny, Valerie knew, was the moment Derek lost his.

Now, she just needed to convince him of that.

As Carla stopped pacing and looked her way, their eyes met briefly, a silent understanding passing between them. Valerie didn't need words to know what came next. It was time. The plan was in motion, and no matter what came of it, there was no turning back. She could only hope that the choice she was about to make would be the one that finally set her free.

"He'll come for you," Carla had warned earlier, her voice unwavering, but there was an edge of concern beneath her calm exterior. "But he's not coming alone."

Valerie's mind had barely processed the words before her body had already tensed. She had known the risks—knew that Derek wouldn't go down without a fight. But hearing it from Carla, the one person who had been by her side through it all, made it feel even more real. She could feel her heart thundering in her chest, a mixture of dread and determination rising up like a tide. It was happening now, faster than she had anticipated. Too fast. And yet, there was no time to hesitate, no time for second thoughts.

She nodded, but the motion felt mechanical, as though her mind were already working a step ahead of her body, calculating the next move. Her thoughts raced, flipping through the details of the plan, the faces of those who had stood by her. She thought of the underground network— those who had given her the tools to finally make a move, the ones who had supplied her with the damning evidence she needed to expose Derek for the monster he truly was. The sordid details of Derek's past, the lies he'd spun, the abuse he'd inflicted—everything he thought he had buried deep, hidden from the world, was now on the verge of coming to light.

Valerie had spent years watching him manipulate and control, believing himself untouchable. She had been his victim for far too long, trapped in the labyrinth of fear he'd built around her. But now, the tables were about to turn. The NEXT system, that sprawling web of influence and power, had no idea what it was about to lose. Valerie had seen the depths of Derek's cruelty firsthand—how he preyed on the vulnerable, how he used his position to destroy those who dared to defy him. She had lived in constant fear, tiptoeing around him, doing whatever it took to avoid his wrath. But that was before. Now, she was the one holding the power. She was the one in control. And Derek would soon understand that he was no longer the one calling the shots.

From the moment Valerie had learned the true extent of NEXT's reach—how deeply its tendrils had woven into every corner of society—she had understood that this battle was about more than just her own freedom. It was no longer simply about breaking free from Derek's grasp. It was about something bigger, something far more important. It was about her children. It was about giving them a future without the looming shadow of fear that had clouded her every decision for years. This wasn't just a fight for her own survival—it was a fight to end the cycle of fear and control that had been passed down for far too long.

The fear that had once paralyzed her now fueled her every step, each movement driven by the knowledge that she wasn't just doing this for herself. She was doing it for them. For Sophie and Mason, the children who had never known a world without fear. She would give them that world. A world where they could grow up without the specter of Derek's cruelty hanging over their heads, a world where they could live, truly live, without the ever-present threat of being torn apart by the system that had kept her chained for so long.

And as the moments stretched out before her, Valerie felt something she hadn't felt in years: hope. It was small, fragile, but it was there. And it was enough.

Carla set down the folder she'd been holding and walked over to Valerie, giving her a steady, knowing look. "You sure about this?"

Valerie exhaled slowly, her gaze fixed on the door. She could almost hear Derek's footsteps in her mind, his voice taunting her as he barged through the threshold. *But not this time.* This time, it would be different.

"I'm done running," Valerie said, her voice stronger than it had ever been. "It ends tonight."

The house was unnervingly still when Derek arrived, the kind of quiet that pressed down on the air, thick and suffocating. It was a silence that seemed to hang in the spaces between breaths, stretching out every second, every movement. And Derek, as oblivious as ever, had no idea that he was stepping into a meticulously crafted trap—one that had been set with precision, with every detail accounted for. The lights above flickered intermittently, a seemingly innocent quirk of the old wiring, but Valerie and Carla had made sure of it. Each flicker was timed, each shadow cast just right to keep him off balance, to make him question his surroundings, his senses. He didn't know it, but the very atmosphere had been tailored to throw him into a state of unease.

The trap was set.

Valerie stood in the far corner of the room, blending into the shadows like a specter, her back pressed firmly against the wall. The revolver was still hidden against her lower back, a reassuring weight that she could feel with every movement, every breath. Her palms were clammy, but her grip was firm, as steady as the resolve that had slowly built inside her over the past few days. Her breath came in shallow, controlled bursts, each exhale a reminder to keep calm, to stay in control. The adrenaline was already coursing through her veins, but she couldn't afford to let it overtake her. There was no room for panic, no room for hesitation. She had no idea how this would play out—what kind of reaction Derek would have when the truth finally came crashing down—but one thing was certain: she wouldn't back down. Not this time. The door slammed open with a violent crash, the sound of the hinges creaking under the force echoing through the house like a war drum, a forewarning that Derek had arrived. Valerie didn't flinch. She didn't even blink. Her gaze remained fixed, unwavering, on the shadows in the doorway. The man who had controlled her life, who had twisted it into something unrecognizable, was finally here. The time for running, for hiding, was over. This was it. Derek stepped into the room, his presence as imposing as ever, his eyes scanning the space, his body tense, as though sensing something was amiss. He couldn't have known how carefully every inch of the room had been prepared for this moment. His focus was on the flickering lights, the silence that now seemed unnatural, but he didn't know it was all a part of the game. Valerie's pulse raced, but her face remained an impassive mask. She had no illusions about what was coming. Derek wouldn't be intimidated by a few lights, but he would be thrown off. And when the time came, when everything was aligned just right, she would make her move. No more running, no more cowering. She was done.

The door was closed behind him with a soft thud, and the weight of the moment hung in the air. Valerie exhaled slowly, her fingers tightening around the revolver's handle, feeling its cool surface against her skin. This wasn't just about survival anymore. This was about power. And for the first time in a long time, Valerie felt it—she wasn't the prey. She was the predator.

He was tall, broad-shouldered, and moved with the same imposing presence that had always commanded attention. Derek carried with him the same aura of authority, the one that had made people bend to his will, that had made Valerie shrink, retreat, and obey. But now, as he stepped into the room, that familiar aura seemed almost comical. Valerie saw him with a clarity that had eluded her for years. He was no longer the man who had terrorized her, the man who had held her life in his hands like it was a game of chess. Now, she saw him for what he truly was—a monster. A grotesque manifestation of everything wrong with the system that had allowed men like him to rise, to rule over others with impunity. The illusion of power he wore so easily was nothing more than a façade, and Valerie had finally peeled it away.

Derek's eyes scanned the room, darting over the shadows, over the faintly flickering lights. When his gaze landed on Valerie, still and unmoving in the corner, his expression hardened, lips curling into a sneer. He didn't say anything at first, just took her in, as though trying to figure out what game she was playing. But the uncertainty that flashed briefly across his face, as he registered the absence of fear in her eyes, was unmistakable. He had been accustomed to seeing her scared, broken, desperate. But not now. Not anymore.

"Well, well," Derek drawled, his voice dripping with condescension. His smile was thin and cruel, stretching across his face in a way that made Valerie's skin crawl, like a snake preparing to strike. "You thought you could hide forever? Thought you could escape me?"

The words were meant to taunt, to remind her of the power he once held over her. But they no longer had the desired effect. Valerie stood tall, her posture unyielding as her gaze locked with his. For a long moment, she said nothing. She let the silence between them grow, let it settle like the thick tension in the room. Derek wanted to see her break, to see her cower. But she wasn't the woman he had once known. She wasn't the woman who had been reduced to silence, to fear, to submission. Finally, Valerie spoke. Her voice was low, steady, but there was a strength to it that cut through the silence like a blade. It was the voice of someone who had lived through the worst and had come out the other side, unbroken, stronger. "You should have learned by now, Derek. You don't control me anymore."

Her words echoed in the stillness, hanging in the air like a challenge thrown into the heart of the storm. There was no fear in them, no hesitation. Only defiance. The sound of her voice—sharp, unwavering—was all it took to shift the dynamic between them, to send a jolt through Derek's chest. For the briefest of moments, his expression faltered. His eyes flickered with something foreign—doubt. It was only for a split second, a fleeting, almost imperceptible moment, but Valerie saw it.

She saw the crack in the wall he had built around himself, the flicker of uncertainty that he quickly masked behind a tightening jaw and a cold stare. In that instant, Valerie realized something she had never dared to hope for: she had done it. She had finally taken back the power. It was hers, not his. She was no longer the prey, and Derek—despite all his strength, despite the years of control—was now standing on the edge of a precipice. She had made him see her. Not the terrified woman who once cowered before him, but someone stronger. Someone who had fought, and who had won. For the first time in years, Valerie felt no fear. He stepped forward, his movements stiff and controlled, the anger radiating off him like heat from a furnace. The room seemed to contract with the force of his presence as he advanced, each step calculated, as if he were testing the ground beneath him, asserting his dominance. "You think you can stand against me? Against everything I've built?" His voice was low, tinged with a mixture of disbelief and fury.

The words landed like a slap, a reminder of the weight of his past and the monstrous empire he had created, but Valerie felt nothing but a surge of cold, determined clarity. She wasn't going to let him intimidate her. Not now. Not ever again.

As Derek closed the distance between them, Valerie's hand moved instinctively, sliding behind her back, her fingers brushing the cold handle of the revolver. She didn't draw it yet. Not yet. She could feel the tension coiling within her like a spring, wound tight and ready to snap. But it wasn't time. She had to wait. She had to make sure everything played out just right. The plan had been set in motion, and she was no longer the one being controlled.

From the depths of her jacket pocket, Carla's voice crackled to life through the walkie-talkie, a quiet but urgent whisper. "He's close. Hold steady."

Valerie's pulse quickened at the sound of Carla's words, a reminder that the trap was almost fully sprung. There was no turning back now. She had chosen this path, and there was no way out except through.

Derek's footsteps grew louder, each one deliberate, each one a reminder of the power he once held over her. But there was something in his movements now, a subtle change. His eyes were darting around the room, catching on the shadows, the stillness in the air. He knew something was different, though he couldn't place it. The shift was too palpable to ignore, like the calm before a storm.

He reached out then, his hand cutting through the air like a blade, his fingers twitching, as if he believed he could snatch control back with a single grasp. But there was nothing left for him to claim. The power had already shifted.

"I'm giving you one chance, Valerie," he said, his voice dripping with condescension, but beneath it, there was a desperate edge. "Come back to me. Come back to what we had."

His words were sharp, an attempt to manipulate, to draw her back into the web he had once woven around her. Valerie felt the heat of his coercion, the weight of his expectation pressing down on her, but she refused to bend. She could feel the walls he had once built around her starting to crack, starting to crumble.

She stood her ground, eyes locked on his, the defiance in her chest like a roaring fire. No. Not this time.

The woman who had been afraid of Derek, the one who had once trembled in his shadow, was gone. The woman standing before him now was stronger than any of the walls he had built. She was the woman who would fight for her children, for her future, no matter what it took.

"I will never go back to you," Valerie said, her voice steady and cold, a declaration that rang through the air like a challenge.

For a moment, there was only silence. Derek's face twisted, and the mask of control he wore cracked, revealing the bitterness that had festered beneath. He scoffed, a low, cruel laugh escaping from his throat. "You think you can win this? You're nothing without me. You'll always be nothing."

His words were sharp, laced with venom, but Valerie didn't flinch. There was no sting to them anymore. She had heard them all before, but they didn't have the same power over her. Not anymore.

That's when it happened.

A loud bang ripped through the tense silence, and in the split second before Derek could react, his body froze. His shoulders tensed, his breath caught in his throat, and his eyes widened in disbelief, as if he hadn't expected it. A shot had rung out—loud, jarring, and decisive—but it hadn't come from Valerie's gun.

CHAPTER THIRTEEN

Stephanie sat at the kitchen table, the warm, golden sunlight spilling through the window, casting a soft glow across the room. The morning air was crisp, a quiet hum of life beyond the walls of the house—cars passing by, birds chirping, people going about their routines—but in this moment, the world outside felt distant, muted, as if it was waiting for her to make a move. She took a slow sip from her coffee mug, letting the warmth settle in her chest. The taste, dark and rich, mirrored her mood—comforting, familiar, but with an undercurrent of something more. She glanced across the table at Marcus, sitting there with his easy smile and effortless confidence. His presence filled the room with a quiet assurance, as if everything he touched naturally fell into place. He was handsome, with sharp features that seemed to belong to a man who'd been sculpted by success itself—high cheekbones, a jawline that could cut glass, eyes that gleamed with a certain self-assurance. There was an air about him, something magnetic that drew people in without effort, something she'd learned to recognize. And now, after everything, he was sitting here, right across from her, the man that the NEXT system had decided was her perfect match. She could almost hear the soft hum of approval from the system itself as if it were cheering her on. Success story, it had called him.

And why wouldn't it? Marcus was the epitome of everything the NEXT system celebrated—handsome, charismatic, successful, and well-liked by everyone who crossed his path. A model citizen, a perfect fit in a society that craved conformity. He was everything Stephanie was supposed to want, everything that was supposed to fill the gaps in her life. And yet, she couldn't quite shake the feeling that her search for something more had led her to this moment, to this person, not as a step forward, but perhaps as a step away from something else entirely.

It wasn't supposed to be like this, she knew. It wasn't supposed to feel like she was simply moving forward in a way that made the past fade into nothingness. But here she was, staring at Marcus and wondering if this was what it meant to be truly 'together,' or if she had just traded one version of herself for another. The NEXT system had worked its magic—at least, that's what everyone said.

After her painful, messy divorce, she had found herself adrift, alone, and unsure of where to go next. The world she had known with her ex-husband was gone, and the pieces of her life that had once seemed so solid had shattered into fragments she couldn't quite put back together. She had no idea where to begin, so she did the only thing that made sense at the time. She posted her ex-husband's name on the

NEXT board. It was a small act of defiance, an acknowledgment of her hurt and a way to take back some control, to show that she could erase the years he had spent taking her for granted. She'd expected it to sting—and it did—but there was a part of her that felt empowered by it, as if that finality was the key to unlocking something better.

For weeks after that, she scrolled through countless profiles, half-heartedly reading through the lives of potential matches, but none of them ever seemed to fit. There was something hollow about it all—the curated smiles, the perfect lives that were as polished and fake as the profiles they came in. She was looking for something, though she couldn't quite define what. Until she saw Marcus's profile.

The moment she stumbled upon it, everything clicked. His interests mirrored hers in a way that felt almost eerie. Their values were aligned, their lifestyles practically identical—like a set of puzzle pieces that fit together seamlessly. His passion for art, her own love for travel, his unwavering belief in success, and her own desire for stability—all of it was there. A world built around shared principles, shared goals.

It wasn't love at first sight, not in the way she had imagined it, but it was close enough. The logical part of her brain said it was just the NEXT system at work—matching her with someone who ticked every box. But as she studied his profile, looked at the photos of him smiling in what looked like perfect moments, something inside her whispered that maybe this was what she had been waiting for, without even realizing it. The world was moving forward, and so was she.

When they were matched, Stephanie felt an overwhelming wave of relief sweep over her, as if the universe had finally recognized her suffering and decided it was time to make things right. For the first time in what felt like forever, she could breathe a little easier. It was as though the weight of her past had been lifted, the constant worry and heartache replaced with the promise of something new, something better. The NEXT system had made its choice, and she had been chosen, paired with Marcus—a man whose life seemed to be everything she had ever wanted. It wasn't just a match; it felt like fate. This was her fresh start, her second chance. No more heartbreak, no more doubting herself or questioning what went wrong in the past. This time, everything was going to be perfect.

The future, in that moment, felt assured. She could imagine it clearly now—weeks and months filled with dinners at the finest restaurants, weekends away in idyllic locations, endless compliments, and gestures of affection that made her feel like the center of his world. She had always dreamed of a life like that. With Marcus, it seemed within reach, right in front of her. All she had to do was embrace it.

But now, sitting across from him, a subtle shift began to settle in, just beneath the surface. At first, it was barely noticeable—an almost imperceptible change that Stephanie tried to ignore, chalking it up to her own overthinking. After all, they were still in the early stages, still learning each other's rhythms. But as the days passed, that feeling grew, something she couldn't quite put her finger on, a sense of unease that tugged at her in the quiet moments. It was like a faint crack in an otherwise perfect façade—something so small it could almost be dismissed, but it was there, growing ever so slightly with every passing day.

Marcus had always been attentive, almost excessively so. At first, it was endearing—his thoughtful gestures, his constant, unwavering attention. He sent her flowers every week, each bouquet more elaborate than the last, his notes filled with words that bordered on poetic. He made dinner reservations at the best restaurants, the ones she'd heard of but never thought she'd have the privilege to visit. He called her every evening, always checking in to see how her day had gone, always listening with genuine interest. It was flattering at first, even comforting. She had never been the object of such constant adoration, and it felt good. He made her feel seen, important, as if she was the only thing that mattered in his world.

But then, the small things began to pile up, and it wasn't long before Stephanie started to feel the weight of them, even if they were subtle at first. His compliments, once charming, began to feel calculated. The flowers, though beautiful, started to arrive with increasing regularity, as if they were a standard part of a ritual that had nothing to do with spontaneity. The dinner reservations, too—each one was carefully selected, but after a while, it felt more like he was going through the motions, checking off a list of things he thought she would appreciate. The conversations, once fluid and engaging, became more structured, as though he were asking questions not to learn about her but to confirm that she fit the mold he had already created in his mind.

She had always believed that attention was a sign of affection, that a man who went out of his way to shower her with praise and gifts was truly invested in her. But now, the attention felt different—almost suffocating. It was as if Marcus was trying to create a version of her, a reflection of what he thought she should be. Every smile, every compliment, every thoughtful gesture was framed in the context of the "perfect match" they were supposed to be, and it started to feel less like genuine love and more like an expectation—one that neither of them had agreed to.

It wasn't that Marcus was doing anything overtly wrong; it was just that something about his actions felt... off. Like he was trying too hard, pushing a vision of a perfect relationship that was based more on his idea of what it should be than on who they really were. And as much as she tried to dismiss the feeling, it lingered—like a faint echo, growing louder each time he made another gesture, each time he overstepped her comfort zone with his overwhelming need to please.

It all started with the small suggestions, the ones that seemed so harmless at first. Marcus would notice the tiniest details about her daily habits—the way she left her shoes near the door after a long day or how she tended to leave the dishes until the evening rather than washing them right away—and gently, almost apologetically, he would offer a little suggestion to change that. He would smile as he made his point, his voice soft and reassuring, as if he were trying to make her life easier, as if he were trying to help her become a better version of herself. At first, Stephanie didn't mind. In fact, she found it thoughtful, even endearing. It was a sign, she thought, that he cared enough to notice the little things, that he was willing to help her streamline her life. She imagined that these were the kinds of things a couple did—help each other improve, make subtle adjustments to live a more harmonious life together. It seemed harmless enough. But then, the suggestions didn't stop. They became more frequent, more specific, until it felt like she was being nudged into a life that wasn't entirely her own. What had once been a casual offer to tidy up the house or rearrange a schedule now felt like a constant stream of reminders—an ongoing series of little nudges meant to gently steer her behavior in a direction that, she couldn't deny, aligned more with Marcus's idea of what was best for them, for their relationship, for their life together.

"Stephanie," Marcus had said one night, the soft light from the lamp casting shadows across his face, as they sat together in their cozy living room, sipping wine. He was leaning forward slightly, his fingers tapping rhythmically on his glass, his smile wide but focused, like he was about to offer an idea that he knew would be just right for her. "I was thinking... maybe we could wake up earlier? You know, start the day with some yoga or meditation. It's been proven to reduce stress, help with focus, and make the day more productive. We could even do it together, just you and me, as a way to center ourselves before the day starts. What do you think?"

Stephanie blinked, slightly taken aback by the sudden suggestion. She hadn't been expecting it—after all, their mornings had always been a bit of a slow start. "Uh, yoga, huh?" she said, hesitating as she took another sip of wine, trying to mask the uncertainty creeping in. "I mean, I've never really been a fan of getting up at 5 a.m. for anything, let alone yoga. You know I'm not exactly a morning person."

Marcus chuckled, his voice soothing, almost coaxing. "I get it, I really do," he said, his tone a little too understanding, as if he were reassuring her that this was something that would be good for them, something she'd come to appreciate. "But think about it—just imagine how much more energy we'd have, how much more focused and productive we could be. It's a small change, but it could really make a difference. And we'd be doing it together, making it a part of our routine. Doesn't that sound like a good way to start our mornings?"

Stephanie took a moment, letting the words sink in. She could already feel a pressure building, the subtle nudge he was offering, the gentle persuasion that had worked so well on her in the past. It wasn't that the idea was entirely bad—it wasn't—but it felt like something was missing, like she was being nudged into a role that didn't quite fit. Still, not wanting to make a fuss, she agreed.

"Okay, I'll give it a try," she said, her voice quieter than she intended, but she didn't want to rock the boat. "We can start tomorrow. But I'm not promising to be all zen and meditative at 5 a.m.," she added with a small laugh, trying to lighten the mood.

Marcus smiled broadly, his eyes sparkling as if he had won a small victory. "Great! I think you'll see the benefits in no time. We're going to feel so much better, you'll see."

But even as he spoke, a small knot formed in Stephanie's stomach. It wasn't that yoga was a bad idea, but something about the way he framed it—like it was just the latest in a string of changes he thought would improve their lives—left her with a sense of unease she couldn't shake. It was as if she were slowly being molded into someone she didn't entirely recognize.

Then, a few nights later, after dinner, Marcus brought up another subject—this time, about their finances.

"You know," he said casually, his voice light but with an edge of finality, "I've been doing some research on the best ways to manage our finances. If you let me handle the investments, I can make sure we have a solid plan for the future. I've got some great ideas on how to grow our savings. We won't have to worry about anything. I'll take care of it."

Stephanie set her fork down, her mouth dry, her pulse quickening. She looked at him, confused, as if trying to understand what he was suggesting. "Wait, what? You want to... handle the investments? I mean, don't you think we should make those decisions together? I've always kept track of our finances before. I thought we were in this together."

Marcus's expression didn't falter, but his tone became smoother, more persuasive. "Of course, I understand that, but look, I've been researching this for a while. I'm really good at this stuff, Stephanie. I know where the market's going, I know the best places to put our money. This is just one less thing for you to worry about. We'll be set up for the future, and you won't have to stress over it. Trust me on this."

There it was again—the certainty, the air of finality in his words that made it clear this wasn't a conversation; it was an offer, one that had already been decided in his mind. "It's not about trust," she said, her voice a little sharper than she intended. "It's about being partners, making these kinds of decisions together."

Marcus leaned back slightly, his fingers lacing together in his lap. His eyes softened, but there was a subtle tension in his jaw. "I get that, I do. But sometimes, we need someone who can take charge of things, someone who can make the tough decisions. And right now, that's me. I just want what's best for us, Stephanie. We'll be in a much better position if I handle this."

Her stomach twisted. It wasn't about the money—it wasn't even about the fact that Marcus might actually be right, that his expertise could help them. It was the way he dismissed her, how he seemed to believe that her thoughts, her input, weren't necessary. It was as if he had already decided what was best for them both, without considering her at all.

"Okay, Marcus," she said, her voice a little flat, her mind racing. "But I need you to understand that I'm still here. I still want to be a part of these decisions."

"I know, I know," he replied quickly, the edge of irritation just barely there. "But this is for the best. Trust me."

Stephanie didn't know what bothered her more—the fact that Marcus assumed control over such an important aspect of their lives without asking for her opinion or the fact that, somehow, she had let him get away with it. It wasn't that she was incapable of managing finances, but she suddenly felt as if her role in their relationship was shifting, becoming less about mutual decision-making and more about him being the one who called the shots. Every suggestion, every comment, every well-meaning nudge felt like another piece of her independence slipping away. And it wasn't just yoga or finances anymore. It was everything.

Stephanie sat still, her fingers curling around the rim of her coffee cup, her mind racing as the unease in her chest expanded. The world outside the window was bright and bustling with the normal rhythm of the day, but inside, everything felt off-kilter. She hadn't expected it to be this way. She had thought that Marcus was the answer to everything—the perfect match, the antidote to the years of pain she had endured. But now, sitting across from him at the kitchen table, she could feel the weight of her doubts pressing down on her.

It wasn't just the suggestion to move away. It wasn't just that Marcus was so determined to push their lives in a direction she hadn't even considered. It was something deeper, something that had been growing quietly in the back of her mind, slowly taking root. Everything in her life, it seemed, had been dictated by him. Every small choice, every routine, every conversation—they had all been shaped by his idea of what was best. The irony didn't escape her.

She had thought the NEXT system had given her control. After her divorce, after the emotional wreckage of years spent with a man who had never really seen her, she had sought refuge in the idea of a perfect match. She had posted her ex-husband's name in the board, a small act of defiance against the man who had never truly understood her. The system had promised her a fresh start, a new life. She had been eager to buy into it, desperate to leave behind the hurt and start anew. She believed that by following the NEXT algorithm, she could find happiness in the arms of someone who perfectly matched her every desire. But now, as she sat there, staring at the man across from her, she wondered if the system had done its job too well. Maybe it hadn't found her a perfect match; it had found her a man who fit its narrow, calculated definition of success.

Marcus was everything the algorithm had promised—handsome, successful, charismatic. He was charming, well-spoken, and always in control. On the surface, he was perfect. He had the right job, the right habits, the right lifestyle. He was a model citizen in every sense of the word. But the more she thought about it, the more Stephanie realized that perfection, at least in Marcus's case, seemed to come with strings attached. Strings that pulled at her in ways she hadn't fully recognized before.

What had seemed like considerate gestures—suggestions about their routine, their health, their finances—were now starting to feel like subtle commands. It wasn't just about what Marcus wanted; it was about what Marcus thought was best for them, for her. His perfect vision of their life was slowly becoming the only reality she knew. It wasn't a partnership anymore. It was more like a carefully constructed performance, where she played her part and he played his. But who was she in all of this? And where did she fit into his meticulously planned life?

Stephanie's gaze shifted to Marcus, who was smiling at her, his eyes soft, as if he could read her thoughts. She felt a pang of guilt—he wasn't a bad man. He was kind, attentive, even loving in his own way. But something about the way he was trying to shape her, to mold their life into something so... flawless, left her feeling suffocated. She had bought into the idea that NEXT was a system that could guide her to true happiness, that it could create the perfect life for her, based on compatibility and shared values. But now she was questioning everything.

Was Marcus really the perfect match? Or had the system just found someone who fit its idea of what success looked like—someone who could make her life seem perfect on the outside, while quietly stripping away the things that truly mattered? The parts of her that weren't so easily defined by algorithms and data points—her quirks, her imperfections, the things that made her who she was.

Her thoughts were interrupted when Marcus reached across the table, his hand resting gently on hers. His touch was warm, comforting even, but it felt different now—like an anchor she wasn't sure she wanted. His smile was reassuring, too perfect, too practiced. "It's going to be amazing, I promise," he said, his voice smooth, almost hypnotic, like a lullaby meant to calm her racing thoughts. "You won't regret it. I know this is the right move for us, for our future."

But Stephanie couldn't shake the nagging feeling that something was wrong. She had believed in the system, had trusted it to lead her to happiness, to peace, to a fresh start. But now, as she looked at Marcus, she was starting to wonder if the system had just found her a man who fit its mold—someone who wasn't really the perfect match, but someone who was perfect for the system's idea of a perfect life. And maybe, just maybe, that was the problem.

She felt a wave of doubt wash over her, the realization creeping in that she might not be in control of her life after all. She had thought that posting her ex-husband's name on the board had been an act of liberation, a way to take charge of her future. But now, it seemed like someone else was taking control of her life for her—someone who didn't understand her, who only saw her as a piece in the perfect puzzle he was creating. She had never wanted to be anyone's project. She had never wanted to feel like she was just another success story, another trophy to be displayed.

As she looked into Marcus's eyes, she could see the certainty in them, the calm assurance that everything was fine, that everything would be just the way it was supposed to be. But Stephanie couldn't ignore the sinking feeling in her chest. She didn't know if she had found a perfect match—or if she had been matched with someone who was perfect for the system's vision of what a life should look like. Either way, it didn't feel like her life anymore.

And maybe, just maybe, that was the problem.

CHAPTER FOURTEEN

Tom and Amanda were the quintessential NEXT success story. They were everything the system promised—a model couple that others aspired to become. To the outside world, they were living proof that the NEXT algorithm worked, the embodiment of its power to craft perfect, harmonious relationships. They were, by all appearances, the epitome of compatibility. They had it all. Their relationship was the gold standard, the one that the system boasted about—the kind of love everyone was supposed to want, a love that was scientifically tailored to fit the algorithm's exacting criteria. Tom and Amanda ran a thriving tech company, their startup having skyrocketed into success. Their personal brand was just as flawless as their business. They were everywhere—on TV, in interviews, speaking at conferences, appearing in magazines. Their faces adorned the covers of lifestyle publications that praised their achievements, both professional and personal. Their social media accounts were nothing less than a glossy parade of perfection: exotic vacation shots from remote islands with turquoise water, charitable galas with A-list celebrities, business meetings with high-profile clients dressed in sharp suits and sleek dresses. The posts were carefully curated, each image a product of meticulous planning. The captions were a symphony of success, ambition, and happiness. Their home—modern, minimalist, and picture-perfect—was a backdrop for countless selfies, always capturing the perfect angles, always smiling, always flawless.

They had money. They had status. They had influence. They had everything that mattered in the world they inhabited, or so it seemed. To anyone watching from the outside, Tom and Amanda were a symbol of what the NEXT system promised—a flawless, unshakable bond that defied the odds, that thrived under the weight of expectations. They were the dream couple, a perfect match, and everyone else was supposed to look at them and say, "That's what I want."

But the problem with perfection was that it had a way of hiding the cracks beneath the surface. What no one saw—what no one could see—was that beneath the polished exterior, Tom and Amanda were not what they seemed. Their relationship had shifted over time, morphing into something far more mechanical than either of them had realized. What started as an undeniable chemistry, a spark that had once drawn them together, had slowly been replaced by something more like a well-oiled machine. They had become business partners more than romantic partners, their lives a series of tasks to be completed, goals to be achieved. There was no time for intimacy, no room for vulnerability. Their connection was based on synergy, efficiency, and shared ambition, not love. The partnership was still functional, at least in the traditional sense. They supported each other's goals, they checked off the boxes of success—both professionally and personally. They were the power couple that everyone admired, the couple everyone believed in. But behind closed doors, it felt different. The warmth that once existed between them had been replaced by something colder, more clinical. They operated as if their relationship was just another project to manage, their love story a brand to be cultivated, marketed, and sold. There was no longer room for genuine affection, for the messy, unpredictable emotions that once connected them. Their intimacy had been traded in for a polished, perfect image, one that could sell to the masses but not one that could sustain the actual bond they once shared.

Tom, always the charismatic frontman, had been the first to notice the change, though he hadn't fully understood what was happening. He'd seen the cracks, but like the world around him, he'd ignored them. Amanda had been the same. She was so focused on maintaining the image, on keeping up the appearance of perfection, that she hadn't stopped to question it. She had told herself it was fine. It was all fine. Their success was fine. Their life was fine. But somewhere in the back of her mind, something had begun to stir. She didn't want to admit it, but she couldn't ignore the feeling of emptiness that had settled into the crevices of her life.

It wasn't until the last big conference, when the applause died down and the cameras turned off, that they both began to notice how distant they had become. They had spoken at the event, given their usual polished answers to the questions from the audience, and smiled for the photographers as if everything was perfect. But as they left the stage, something was different. The air between them had thickened with unspoken tension. Tom had glanced at Amanda, who was now scrolling through her phone, her fingers tapping absentmindedly. For the first time in a long while, he felt a twinge of something unsettling in his chest— a feeling he couldn't quite place. It wasn't anger or resentment, but it was something close. He opened his mouth to say something, anything, but the words caught in his throat. He couldn't ask her how she felt about their life— about the fact that they hadn't really lived it together for years.

Amanda felt it too. She had always been so caught up in their public image, so focused on keeping the machine running smoothly, that she hadn't noticed how distant they had grown. She thought she had everything under control. She had convinced herself that their success was enough to fill the void, to make everything feel meaningful. But now, in the quiet after the applause, the silence between them felt like a heavy weight.

She looked at him, really looked at him, for the first time in months. There was something about his eyes, the way they seemed to search hers, that made her stomach turn. For a moment, the polished façade of their relationship cracked, and she saw him—really saw him—as a person, not just as a business partner or an image to maintain.

Amanda sat at her desk, the sleek, modern office around her feeling more like a cage than a place of success. The glass walls framed the city below, but her gaze was unfocused, distant. The weight of the morning's tension pressed heavily on her chest, a constant reminder that something was wrong. The email draft in front of her was a perfect representation of the life she had been living—polished, professional, and utterly detached from reality. It was an invitation to an exclusive NEXT gala, an event where she and Tom were scheduled to shine as the poster couple for the system that had supposedly transformed their lives.

The words in the email were a rehearsed narrative, all about branding, image, and maintaining the illusion of their perfect life. Amanda's stomach churned as she read them. The gala wasn't just a chance to attend a glamorous event—it was a platform for them to solidify their status as the ultimate success story, a perfect match made by the NEXT algorithm. They were to give a speech, touting how NEXT had brought them together, how it had led to their business triumphs, and how it was the foundation of their flawless relationship.

For weeks, Tom had been obsessed with the details of the speech. He'd talked about how they'd position themselves as "the face of the future of relationships," how they would highlight their success as proof that the NEXT system was the answer to every relationship problem. Every element had been planned out with the precision of a military operation—from their matching outfits to their synchronized movements on stage, even the anecdotes they'd share about their early days together. Every word, every gesture, was meant to create the perfect image, the perfect performance. There was no room for authenticity, no room for deviation from the script.

Tom had already begun rehearsing his lines—running them over and over, polishing them until they were as smooth as the glass desk Amanda now sat at. His passion for the performance was palpable, as it always was. He had a gift for turning their lives into a show, an act designed to impress and inspire. He was always the one in the spotlight, the one who knew how to craft an image, to mold their lives into something that could be sold to the world. And Amanda, for so long, had played along. She had followed his lead, stepping into her role as the perfect partner, the perfect woman to complement his perfect vision.

But today, as she sat alone in her office, the suffocating weight of it all finally hit her. The reality that she had been living in for so long, the one that had seemed so seamless and natural, now felt like a prison. She had spent so many years burying her doubts, convincing herself that this was what she wanted, that this was the dream life they had built together. But now, it was all falling apart at the seams.

Amanda had always known something was missing, but she had never allowed herself to confront it—until now. The act, the performance, the perfect image they had so carefully constructed—it wasn't enough anymore. She was tired of pretending. She was tired of being a pawn in the game Tom had set up, of playing her part in a story that wasn't even hers. She had been living for the applause, living for the validation that came from being part of the NEXT narrative, but it had never filled the void inside her. She had been so focused on maintaining the façade of perfection that she had forgotten what it felt like to be real.

Her fingers hovered over the keyboard, and for a moment, she wondered if she should cancel their participation in the gala, if she should tell Tom that she couldn't go through with it. But the thought of upsetting him, of breaking the carefully constructed image they had built, paralyzed her. Tom was counting on her to play her part, to make everything look flawless. He needed her to be the perfect wife, the perfect business partner, the perfect match.

But Amanda couldn't do it anymore. The idea of standing on that stage, presenting herself as the epitome of the NEXT success story, felt suffocating. She was tired of pretending to be someone she wasn't. She didn't want to be the face of a system that had promised perfection but had failed to deliver anything real.

Her mind raced, her heart pounding in her chest. She had spent so much of her life trying to please Tom, trying to maintain the illusion that their relationship was something it wasn't, trying to live up to the expectations of a system that cared more about image than substance. But now, the weight of all those years of pretending, of keeping up the act, was too much to bear.

Amanda took a deep breath and closed her eyes. The decision was terrifying. She didn't know what it would mean for her and Tom, or for their business, or for the image they had built. But deep down, she knew she couldn't keep living this way. She couldn't keep sacrificing herself for the sake of a perfect picture that wasn't even real.

She deleted the email draft, watching the cursor blink on the empty screen. The weight on her chest eased slightly, but only just. It was a small act, but it felt like the first step in reclaiming her life, in stepping away from the narrative that had been written for her.

Amanda stared at the blank screen, feeling a strange mix of relief and fear. There was no going back now. She had crossed a line, and for the first time in a long time, she wasn't sure where it would lead.

In the midst of the turmoil that had overtaken Amanda's mind, she reached out to Jenna, her closest friend—someone who had known her long before NEXT had ever entered the picture. Jenna was the one person who could still see her for who she truly was, not the polished, perfect version of herself that the world and Tom expected. Jenna had been a constant, a grounding force, even when Amanda had become entangled in the manufactured image of success that NEXT had helped create. Tonight, Amanda needed that connection more than ever.

The two of them sat at a small table in a cozy wine bar, dimly lit and filled with the soft hum of conversation from other patrons. A bottle of red sat between them, glasses half-filled, but neither of them seemed interested in refilling just yet. Amanda, her eyes distant, was stirring her wine slowly, barely aware of the action as her thoughts raced.

She took a long breath, gathering the courage she had lacked for weeks, and finally spoke, her voice barely rising above a whisper, as if the admission itself might break something within her.

"I'm thinking of leaving him," she confessed, her gaze dropping to her glass, unable to meet Jenna's eyes. Her fingers fidgeted with the rim of her glass, a nervous tick she hadn't indulged in since before NEXT had taken over her life.

Jenna's eyes widened in shock, and she leaned in, her voice sharp with concern. "You're serious?" she asked, her tone edged with disbelief. "But what about everything you've built? The company? Your life together? You can't just walk away from that, Amanda. Not after everything."

Amanda shifted uncomfortably, her fingers still tracing the edge of the glass as she considered her words carefully. She wasn't sure what was harder—saying it out loud or hearing it in her own mind. "I know," she replied, her voice flat. "But what if this is it? What if this is the best it's ever going to get, and it's not enough? What if I've already sacrificed too much just to keep this picture-perfect life going?"

The words hung heavy in the air, unspoken truths drifting between them like smoke. Jenna watched her for a long moment, her expression softening as she processed what Amanda had said. She had always known Amanda as someone driven by ambition, someone who had built her life alongside Tom with a fierce determination to succeed, to prove that they were the best. They had everything, everything that the world said mattered—wealth, status, a thriving business. But here, in the silence between them, Amanda's vulnerability was on full display.

Jenna exhaled slowly, the weight of the conversation settling on her shoulders. "You know that leaving him isn't just about walking away from him, right?" she said quietly, her voice losing some of its sharpness. "It's about walking away from everything you've built together. The company. The wealth. The life you've been living. You can't pretend that won't be a huge risk."

Amanda's chest tightened at the thought. She hadn't fully allowed herself to think about what walking away would mean—how it wasn't just a rejection of Tom, but a rejection of the life she had worked so hard to create. Leaving a NEXT match was more than just leaving a person. It was about stepping away from a carefully constructed empire, a life that had been meticulously sculpted to be the ideal, the envy of others. It meant walking away from the image of perfection they had both curated, the kind of life that people only dreamed about. But the truth was, that life had stopped feeling like hers a long time ago.

"I know it would mean losing everything," Amanda said, the words slipping from her mouth with a heaviness that made them feel final. She couldn't bring herself to look at Jenna, her gaze fixed on her glass, watching the wine swirl as though it might offer some clarity. "But what if the life we've built isn't enough anymore? What if I've already sacrificed who I really am for this... for this image? What if I'm not really living, but just existing in the shadow of this perfect story we've created? Is that worth it?"

Jenna took a deep breath, letting the silence stretch for a moment before responding. "You know you'll have to rebuild everything, right? It's not just the company or the status—it's the whole life. Starting over from scratch. It's going to be hard."

Amanda finally met her eyes, and for the first time in a long time, she felt a flicker of clarity. Jenna's words were blunt, but they were also the reality Amanda had been trying to avoid. She knew she would have to walk away from everything—her business, her wealth, and the ideal life she had been living. She knew the price. But the price of staying, of continuing to live a lie, felt worse than anything she could imagine.

"I know," she replied softly, her voice barely above a murmur. "I don't even know where I'd start. But maybe that's what I need. Maybe I need to stop trying to fit into this perfect mold and start being real again. Even if it means losing everything."

The weight of the decision was still heavy, but for the first time, it felt like it was her decision. It wasn't the NEXT system's, and it wasn't Tom's. It was hers, and that realization felt like a small victory. As she sat there, her heart still racing, Amanda knew that walking away wasn't going to be easy. But it was the only choice left.

CHAPTER FIFTEEN

Kara sat on the edge of her bed, the glow of her phone casting a dull light in the otherwise dark room. The screen flickered with the familiar interface of the NEXT app, its red borders sharp and cold. The list of potential matches seemed to mock her now, each profile more like an item in a catalog than a real person. The app promised endless possibilities—swipe right for a new chance at love, swipe left for another mistake. But lately, the game had lost its appeal. She had gone through this process so many times before. The brief flurry of excitement when a new match popped up, the empty interactions that followed—messages of polite interest, casual exchanges that never went beyond surface-level small talk. Each partner felt like a fleeting moment, a distraction, but nothing more. She would post a partner, receive a few comments of encouragement, and then quietly move on when the connection faded. But recently, even the comfort of familiarity had lost its allure. The relationships that were supposed to bring some kind of fulfillment now seemed like hollow echoes of something real.

Kara's mind drifted back to her most recent match— Jeremy. At first, he had seemed promising. Tall, with the kind of rugged handsomeness that turned heads, and that dangerous charisma that made people sit up and take notice. He wasn't the type you'd expect to see on a platform like NEXT. He was the kind of guy you might see at a dive bar, leaning against the counter, his eyes scanning the crowd like he didn't care whether anyone noticed him or not. But he had noticed her. And she had noticed him, too.

Their time together had started off with the thrill of something new—weekends spent exploring the city, taking impulsive walks through the parks, trying out new food trucks, sharing cheap wine and stolen moments. There were stories exchanged between them, stories of heartbreaks, of regrets, of small victories and lost opportunities. He had seemed like someone who understood, who could fill the void she had grown so used to, the void NEXT promised to fill with perfect matches.

But now, as she sat on her bed, staring at the notification that flashed on her screen—a match request from Jeremy—Kara felt nothing. Not surprise, not disappointment, just a dull sense of inevitability. It was like she could see the cycle unfolding before her. She'd known this moment was coming. She'd seen him eyeing the NEXT board for a new partner long before their six-month milestone had come and gone. Six months. It was supposed to be the mark of something lasting, a sign that they had made it past the honeymoon phase. But to Kara, it was just another reminder of how well NEXT worked—how easily it churned through relationships like some kind of factory line, producing perfectly tailored matches with an efficiency that left little room for anything real. She had convinced herself that Jeremy was different at first. But now, the idea of continuing on with him, of pretending this was all meaningful, felt like a lie. Every interaction with him had felt like a performance, a part of the charade they were both playing. The curated photos, the matching profiles, the endless routine of impressing each other with how perfect they were—was this really the future of love? Was this all there was?

Kara opened the app, hesitated, and then clicked on Jeremy's profile. His picture flashed up—him grinning from ear to ear, a confident smirk that spoke of someone who didn't need to try too hard. And yet, in that moment, Kara found herself asking the question that had been plaguing her for months: Is this all there is?

She swiped through his messages, the ones they'd exchanged over the past few days, the same familiar small talk—plans for dinner, vague mentions of work, no real substance, no deeper connection. She'd convinced herself that they were building something real, but it was all surface-level, all based on the promises NEXT had sold her.

The match request flashed again, a soft ping drawing her back to the screen. She could accept it, move forward with the same routine. She could keep pretending that Jeremy was the answer, that this was her life now. Or... she could let it go. She could walk away from the system, from the fake matches and the artificial connections, and face the uncomfortable, messy truth of starting over. Kara's finger hovered over the screen. She was tired—tired of the expectations, tired of the carefully curated lives, tired of the constant push for perfection. She wasn't sure what the next step was, but for the first time in a long while, she wasn't sure she wanted to play the game anymore.

With a deep breath, she slid her finger across the screen, rejecting the match request. The notification disappeared, and for a brief moment, she felt a strange sense of relief. She didn't know what came next, but at least, for now, she had made the decision for herself. Not for the system. Not for the algorithm. Just for Kara.

Kara stared at Jeremy's profile for a moment longer, the image of him grinning back at her, his eyes glinting with that same careless confidence that had once drawn her in. He was carefree, detached, and she had been, too. The realization hit her hard—she had become just like him. The same nonchalance, the same easy switching between partners, the same hollow promises of something better just around the corner.

But what if the "next" wasn't the answer anymore?

She had seen it too many times before: people moving on without a second thought, as if love could be discarded the same way you would a used product. It had all become a transaction. Swipe, post, match. The algorithm told you what to want, when to want it, and how to dispose of what no longer fit. Each match was supposed to be better than the last, the perfect fit, the ideal partner just waiting to appear. But when did it stop being about connection? When had it all turned into something that felt less like love and more like a game?

Kara's fingers twitched over her phone screen, her thumb poised to either accept or reject the request. She was so tired of the cycle. The first few matches had been fun— exciting, even. There had been novelty in it, the thrill of the unknown. But now, every match felt like the same thing over and over again. Every connection, every fleeting moment, seemed to slip away before it could truly mean anything. All she had to show for it was an endless series of profiles and messages, with no depth to any of them.

The irony wasn't lost on her—this was supposed to be the future of love. A system that promised to make relationships easier, more efficient. But instead, it had stripped away what made love feel real in the first place. The thrill of meeting someone new, yes, but also the vulnerability of working through tough times, of compromising, of building something that wasn't perfect but was genuine. The NEXT system didn't promise that. It promised efficiency, success, compatibility. It promised perfection.

But now, staring at Jeremy's face, she realized that perfection didn't matter if it didn't feel like anything. She couldn't keep playing this game. She couldn't keep pretending. The system made it too easy to move on, too easy to discard someone when the novelty wore off. But it also made it too easy to never truly commit, to never put in the work to make something real.

"What happened to working through things?" she whispered to herself again, the words thick with frustration.

She had been caught in the cycle for too long. The constant chase for the next match, the next best thing, never giving any of the relationships the time to breathe, the space to evolve. The reality was that love was messy, uncomfortable, and sometimes downright hard. But the NEXT system wasn't built for that. It wasn't built to help people navigate those complexities. It was built for convenience, for the promise of ease. And ease, she now realized, wasn't worth it if it meant sacrificing what really mattered.

Her heart ached, but there was clarity in the ache. For the first time in a long while, Kara understood what she had been missing. It wasn't the perfect match that mattered. It was the effort. The willingness to face the messiness of life and love, the willingness to put in the work to make something real. She didn't want a "next." She didn't want a perfect match that only existed because an algorithm said it was perfect.

She wanted something real.

With a deep breath, Kara swiped left, rejecting Jeremy's request. It felt like a small victory, but also a painful one. She wasn't sure what she was looking for anymore, but she knew it wasn't this. Not the next perfect match, not the next easy out.

It was something more. Something harder, but more meaningful. She didn't know if she was ready to find it just yet, but for the first time in a long while, she knew she didn't have to keep playing the game.

Kara stared at the phone, the notification still flashing on the screen, taunting her with its relentless promise of compatibility. "You're 98% compatible with Taylor. New match!" The words felt hollow now, like a slap in the face. She could already hear the familiar, soothing voice of the NEXT system in her head: "Here's your perfect match. Keep swiping. Keep searching. Keep moving." But it wasn't perfect. It was just another name, another set of expectations, another cycle that never seemed to end.

She could almost hear the clock ticking in the background, each notification an insistence on moving faster, progressing through life like it was all just a series of transactions. But it didn't feel like progress. It felt like running on a treadmill, frantically trying to get somewhere while the world around her blurred into the same dull monotony.

Kara let out a frustrated sigh and dropped the phone beside her, the weight of it feeling more like a burden than a connection. She wanted to throw it across the room. She wanted to delete everything—her profile, the app, the entire system that had built a cage around her life. But she knew it wasn't that simple.

The system had become too ingrained in the world she lived in, too entrenched in the way people defined relationships now. The more she thought about it, the more it felt like there was no escape. It was everywhere—on her social media, in her conversations, in the eyes of the people she met. They all lived by the NEXT code, this unspoken agreement that love and connection were things to be matched, measured, and constantly refined. Walking away now would be like stepping off the edge of a cliff. There would be nothing left to hold onto, no safety net to catch her. And without it, she'd be adrift. An outcast in a world that didn't know how to function without the NEXT algorithm to guide them.

The thought of it filled her with a quiet desperation. She didn't want to be a part of the game anymore, but what was she supposed to do? What was there left to cling to if she walked away?

Kara sank deeper into the pillows, the weight of the decision pressing down on her. She closed her eyes, trying to shut out the constant hum of the notifications, the ping ping of the algorithm at work. The pressure to match, to meet expectations, to succeed. Was this really the future? Was this really how people were supposed to connect, or was she just too disillusioned to see the point anymore? She thought back to the moments when things had felt real— before the system, before the swiping and posting and matching. There had been relationships that didn't feel like they were governed by an algorithm, relationships that had been messy, complicated, and imperfect. But those had been few and far between, scattered among the noise of the perfectly curated profiles and the flawless facades people put up to impress others.

What happened to just being with someone? she thought bitterly. What happened to getting to know someone for who they truly were, not how they were rated or scored?

A sudden wave of regret washed over her. She had played the game, gone along with the system, hoping that the next match would be the one that finally made sense. But now, it felt like the system had her in its grip, like she was just another cog in its endless, spinning wheel. There was no room for mistakes, no room for imperfection, just a constant push to keep moving forward.

Kara sat up, grabbing her phone again. Her fingers hovered over the screen, unsure of what to do. Taylor, the latest match, was just another name. Another face. Another promise that would eventually be discarded when the novelty wore off. But maybe that was the point, wasn't it? The system wasn't designed for connection—it was designed to keep you hooked, to keep you swiping, always searching for something better, something that never truly existed.

With a heavy heart, Kara made a decision. She didn't swipe right. She didn't swipe left. She closed the app entirely. She had been so consumed by the system, so desperate for a connection that she had let it define her every move. But no more. She wasn't going to keep playing. She wasn't going to let the system control her, not anymore.

For the first time in a long while, Kara felt a flicker of hope—a small, quiet rebellion. It wasn't much, but it was enough to give her some space to breathe. The game would go on without her, but maybe, just maybe, she could start building something real. Something that didn't have to be quantified or measured, something that didn't require her to constantly chase the next match.

The first step wasn't finding someone new—it was learning to be okay with herself again. And for now, that was enough.

David moved through the night like a shadow, his footsteps silent on the cold, cracked pavement. He had been running for weeks, maybe longer—time blurred when you were always looking over your shoulder. Every rustle of a passing car, every footstep behind him made his heart race. It wasn't just the NEXT enforcement agents he was avoiding now; it was the system itself, a relentless machine that would stop at nothing to crush those who threatened it.

His new life was a series of borrowed spaces, forgotten corners of the city where he could disappear for a few days before moving on. A safe house here, a contact there—nothing permanent. There were no roots, no comfort. He had learned to live like a ghost, unseen and unnoticed. The worst part? He was starting to get used to it. But as much as he tried to isolate himself, there were whispers of a growing resistance. The underground network was getting more organized, fueled by those who, like him, had grown sick of the control NEXT wielded over every aspect of their lives. The rebels were scattered, some still unsure of the scope of their power, others already planning how they could dismantle the system piece by piece. David had become their symbol, their leader, but he wasn't sure how much longer he could keep running, let alone lead a revolution.

That night, he was heading to an old warehouse on the outskirts of town. The dim lights were a beacon for those who had made the same choice he had—who had decided to break free. Inside, Trevor Kline was waiting.

Trevor had been one of the few who had survived the car crash—the one David barely escaped from when the NEXT agents had been hot on his trail. They'd crossed paths before, but now, Trevor was different. His eyes were sharp, focused. The accident had left its scars, but it had also hardened him in ways David hadn't expected. Trevor had become a kind of underground investigator, sifting through the wreckage of NEXT's influence, pulling on threads until the whole, ugly system began to unravel.

David found Trevor in the back of the warehouse, a small group of rebel operatives gathered around him. The low murmur of their conversation stopped when David entered. He could feel their eyes on him, some in awe, others with the wariness of people who didn't know whether to trust him yet.

"David," Trevor greeted him, his voice low but strong. "We've got a lot to talk about."

David didn't sit down. He couldn't afford to get too comfortable, not yet. He glanced around the room. "What's going on?" he asked, keeping his tone steady.

Trevor motioned for him to come closer, pointing to a pile of files on a nearby table. "We've been digging into NEXT for a while now. You wouldn't believe what we've found."

David raised an eyebrow. "Try me."

Trevor opened a file and flipped it toward David. "They've been manipulating matches. On purpose. It's not just about pairing people—it's about profit. They deliberately set people up for failure. Partners who are completely incompatible, who are bound to break up. The constant reshuffling, the back-and-forth, that's where the money is."

David stared at the files, the weight of Trevor's words sinking in. "They're not even trying to help people find love anymore. They're just using the system to line their pockets."

"Exactly," Trevor said. "They've been doing it for years. But that's not the worst part."

David's stomach dropped. "What's worse than that?"

Trevor leaned in, his voice dropping to a whisper. "I've uncovered a way to bring the whole damn thing down. All of it. The matches, the system, the control... Everything."

David's heart skipped a beat. For a moment, he just stared at Trevor, as if he hadn't heard him right. "You're telling me we can take them down?"

Trevor nodded. "It's risky. But it's possible. If we can get the right information to the right people, we can expose everything. The manipulation, the fraud... We'll shut down the NEXT system once and for all."

David paced back and forth, the weight of what Trevor was suggesting pressing on him. He had spent months running, staying one step ahead of NEXT, and now Trevor was asking him to step back into the lion's den. He'd always known it wouldn't be easy, but the thought of going head-to-head with the system again felt like a suicide mission.

"What do we have to lose?" Trevor continued. "This is it. This is the chance to end the whole thing. But it's going to take everything we've got."

David rubbed his eyes, trying to focus. The stakes were higher now. They weren't just fighting for freedom anymore—they were fighting to destroy a system that had turned relationships into commodities. A system that had taken too much from too many people.

He looked at the files again. "So, what's the plan?"

"We've got contacts in the right places," Trevor explained. "We just need you to get us the last piece. The final key. And that's where the real danger is."

David nodded grimly. He knew what that meant. But he couldn't back down now—not when they were this close to pulling the plug on NEXT.

"Alright," David said, his voice steady. "Let's burn this system to the ground."

The room filled with a tense silence, but the air was electric with determination. They were in this together now. And if they were going to fight, they would do it on their terms. The war was just beginning.

Isabella sat in the quiet of her apartment, staring out the window at the city's skyline, her mind adrift in a sea of doubts. She had everything she was supposed to want—a perfect life by NEXT's standards. Ethan was everything she could have asked for: charming, successful, considerate, and, above all, kind. They were the poster couple for the system, the ones people admired, the ones who seemed to have it all. They'd been matched for over a year, and their relationship was seen as a triumph—a flawless success story that NEXT paraded across advertisements, billboards, and commercials.

But as the days passed, Isabella began to feel something she hadn't anticipated: a creeping unease.

Her mother had always been skeptical of NEXT. "It's not real love, darling," she would say, her voice tinged with the bitterness of someone who had seen too much. "Love is something you choose. It's not something a system can match for you." At the time, Isabella had brushed off her mother's warnings. What did her mother know about this kind of love? She hadn't grown up with the advancements of technology, the perfect compatibility algorithms that promised to find someone you were meant to be with.

But now, sitting in the silence of her apartment, Isabella wasn't so sure.

Ethan had been nothing but supportive. He had loved her in the way that a perfect match should—thoughtful, patient, with a smile that always seemed to reassure her. They had shared everything, from their favorite meals to their future dreams. And yet, something was missing. There were no moments of rawness, no thrill of discovery. It was like everything had been mapped out for her, every step guided by the invisible hand of NEXT. Even their proposal had felt choreographed, like it was just the next logical step, as if they were following a script that had already been written for them.

She thought about it for a long time. Could it be that the system had made the decision for her? Could it be that the love she was living wasn't really her choice, but just the result of a mathematical calculation?

Isabella's fingers absently traced the rim of her coffee mug as she replayed her thoughts. She had never had the chance to meet someone outside the system. What would that have been like? To find someone the way her mother had—organically, by accident, or by simply being in the right place at the right time? Would the chemistry be different, more real, more hers?

The nagging feeling wouldn't go away.

She thought back to the early days of her match with Ethan, when everything felt fresh and exciting. But that had been before the cameras, before the advertisements. Before NEXT had claimed ownership of their story and plastered it all over the public eye. Once they were featured as the perfect couple, the pressure to live up to that image became suffocating. She felt like she was playing a role, like she had to constantly be the perfect partner in this "perfect match" or risk the system failing them both.

And it wasn't just her feeling conflicted. Ethan was perfect on paper, but was that enough? Could perfection replace what was truly necessary for a lasting connection? She wasn't sure anymore.

Then one evening, as they were sitting at their favorite restaurant—a place they'd been to dozens of times—Ethan let something slip. It was a casual comment, a mention of an ex-girlfriend, and Isabella froze. He didn't seem to think much of it. But Isabella's mind raced.

"Wait, you've had an ex?" she asked, trying to mask the sudden tension in her voice.

Ethan looked at her with a soft smile, a little too relaxed. "Oh, yeah, it was ages ago. Before we were matched. It was nothing serious, just a phase I went through. You know how it is."

Isabella nodded, but her mind was already spinning. An ex. One who hadn't made it onto the NEXT board. A relationship that had never been deemed worthy of being part of their perfect, curated story. How many other things were being hidden from her? How many parts of Ethan's life had never been shared because NEXT had decided they didn't fit the narrative?

She excused herself from the table, stepping out onto the balcony for some air. The cool evening breeze did little to calm her racing thoughts. She stood there for a long time, looking out at the lights of the city. Was this what true love was supposed to feel like? Was it supposed to be easy, guided, with no bumps or surprises?

Her phone buzzed in her pocket, and she pulled it out to see a message from her mother: "Are you sure this is what you want, sweetheart? Don't let a system decide for you."

Her heart clenched. Her mother had been right. But now, it felt like there was no turning back. The entire trajectory of her life had been shaped by a system that promised certainty, but at the cost of her own voice, her own desires.

Isabella went back inside, trying to mask the storm brewing inside her. Ethan didn't notice anything amiss as they resumed their dinner, their conversation drifting back to the surface-level topics they usually discussed. But beneath the veneer of calm, Isabella knew that something was irrevocably different. She couldn't ignore the truth any longer: the life she was living, the love she had, had never been hers to choose.

The NEXT system had given her everything, but at what cost?

Valerie sat in the corner of the dimly lit room, her back pressed against the cold, unyielding wall of the safe house. She tried to steady her breathing, to calm the racing thoughts that assaulted her mind, but it was no use. Her head ached from the endless pressure of running, of never being able to settle. Every shadow seemed like a threat. Every knock at the door sent her heart into overdrive. The kids were sleeping in the room next door—at least, she hoped they were. They hadn't said much lately, just clung to her with silent, fearful eyes. Olivia, her youngest, had barely spoken since they'd been on the move. And Ben, her eldest, was becoming withdrawn, his anger simmering just beneath the surface. They were both too young to understand the full weight of the danger they were in, but Valerie could see it in the way they looked at her, in the way they couldn't sleep without checking the windows or the locks, as if even the house itself couldn't protect them.

She felt like a failure. She had always promised herself that she'd protect them—keep them safe. But what good was safety when she was constantly putting them at risk by dragging them from place to place? She tried to remind herself that she was doing this for them—that exposing the corruption of NEXT and getting away from Derek's control was the right thing. But every time she looked into her children's eyes, the guilt crushed her.

She stood up, pacing the small room, trying to work out the next move in her head. They had barely been at this safe house for a few days. She didn't dare get too comfortable. It never lasted long. The underground network had done their best to help her stay off the radar, but Valerie knew it was only a matter of time before Derek found her again. She had seen the way he operated, the way he could worm his way through the cracks of the system, his power and influence creeping into every corner of their lives. It wasn't enough to just run anymore—Derek was always a step ahead.

Then her phone buzzed, cutting through the silence like a lightning bolt.

It was a message from an unknown number.

"Derek has posted a 'missing person' alert. He's using NEXT's system against you. Be careful."

Valerie's heart stopped. She quickly scanned the message, her mind racing. Derek had done it—he had taken their fight to the NEXT platform, painting her as a criminal. The system, designed to monitor and enforce the relationships it created, had become her worst enemy. It was an unfortunate irony. NEXT had once promised to bring people together, but now it was being used as a weapon to tear her apart.

She opened her browser, quickly navigating to the NEXT platform, heart pounding in her chest. The alert was everywhere. The headline read: "Dangerous Woman Kidnaps Children: Valerie Kline on the Run."

Beneath it was a photo of her, taken at one of the family events she'd attended years ago, a moment that now seemed like a lifetime ago. The words "kidnapped," "dangerous," and "criminal" leapt off the screen, a direct attack on her character. Valerie gripped her phone, her hands trembling. This was bad—really bad. The system had the power to flag people like her as criminals, and once that happened, she knew there was no escaping it. NEXT enforcement agents were already on her trail. They would stop at nothing to bring her back to Derek, to force her into submission, to return her children to his custody. She couldn't let that happen.

Just as she was about to shut down the screen in panic, another message popped up. An anonymous one.

"Derek has found a way to use the NEXT system to legally regain custody of your kids. He's filed a claim. You need to act fast."

The words hit her like a punch to the gut. The last thing she had expected was for Derek to use the system itself to get his hands back on their children. If he had found a loophole, a legal way to bypass everything she'd done to protect them, she didn't know how much longer she could hold on.

She paced the room, her mind spinning, heart racing. How had Derek found this opening? Had he been working with the system this whole time, using it as a weapon to control their lives from the inside? Valerie was starting to wonder if she'd ever truly escaped. Was the NEXT system so deeply embedded in their lives that no matter how far she ran, it could still track her every move?

"Mom..." Ben's voice, low and hesitant, broke her thoughts. She turned to see him standing in the doorway, his face pale, his eyes wide with worry. He was trying to be brave, but she could see the fear in his gaze. He knew something was wrong.

Valerie dropped her phone onto the table and pulled her son into her arms, holding him tight. "It's okay, Ben. I'm not going anywhere. We're going to be alright." But she wasn't sure if that was true. She wasn't sure of anything anymore.

As she held him, her mind raced through her options. She had to find a way to fight back, to expose Derek for the manipulative, controlling person he was. But to do that, she would have to go up against NEXT itself—against a system that had already proven it could take everything from her.

The weight of the task seemed impossible, but she couldn't give up. Not now. Not when the stakes were so high.

She kissed Ben's forehead, whispering reassurances she didn't believe herself, knowing that in the back of her mind, the clock was ticking. They were running out of time.

Amanda stood in front of the mirror, staring at her reflection with a cold, distant look. She barely recognized herself anymore. Her face was a mask of exhaustion, her eyes tired from months of pretending. The woman staring back at her was no longer the ambitious, vibrant partner of a successful entrepreneur. She was someone trapped in a gilded cage, with her every move dictated by a system that promised success at the cost of her own happiness. Tom had always been charming, ambitious, driven—but now she could barely stand to be in the same room with him. Their marriage had once been full of excitement, hope, and the thrill of shared dreams. But that had changed the moment NEXT entered their lives. The system had promised them a perfect, prosperous future—so long as they stayed in line.

Amanda had always known there were strings attached, that their "perfect match" was more about public image than personal connection. But she had played along, kept her doubts hidden, and focused on the bigger picture: their company, their success. The next big deal. The constant praise from the public.

But lately, something inside her had snapped. She was tired of playing the role of the perfect wife, the perfect NEXT couple. She was tired of pretending that everything was fine when all she felt was suffocated.

She had waited too long to confront Tom, but today, there was no avoiding it any longer.

"Tom," she said, her voice steady but firm as she walked into his office, where he sat hunched over a pile of papers, clearly deep in thought. She could hear the low hum of his phone vibrating with constant notifications—the latest reports, the brand endorsements, the social media updates. It was all business, all the time.

He glanced up, his expression unchanged. "What is it now, Amanda? I'm in the middle of something."

She took a deep breath, gathering her resolve. "We need to talk. About us."

Tom's eyes narrowed, his lips curling into a slight frown. "Not now, Amanda. I'm busy. We can talk later."

But Amanda wasn't backing down this time. She stepped forward, shutting the door behind her with a soft click. "No, Tom. It's now or never. I'm tired of pretending. I'm tired of playing this game with you, with NEXT. I don't want to be your perfect match anymore. I don't want to be a part of this system anymore."

Tom sat up straighter, a flicker of annoyance crossing his face. "What are you talking about? You're being ridiculous. We've built this empire together. This—this brand—it's our future. Do you really want to throw it all away over some... some passing feeling?"

Amanda's heart pounded. "It's not a passing feeling, Tom. I'm not happy. I'm suffocating. I've been pretending to be the perfect wife, the perfect NEXT couple, but I can't keep doing this. I can't keep pretending that everything's fine when I'm dying inside. I want out."

Tom's face darkened, and for a moment, Amanda could see the person he really was—the man she'd once admired, now twisted by his own ego. He was the man who cared more about his public image, about the brand they had built, than about her, than about their marriage.

"You're not going anywhere," Tom said coldly, his tone turning manipulative. "If you leave now, it's not just our marriage that's at stake. It's everything we've worked for. The company. The investors. The future. You'll ruin us. You'll ruin yourself. Do you really want to do that, Amanda? For what? A fleeting idea that you want to 'find yourself'? You're smarter than this."

Amanda felt the anger welling up inside her. She had seen this before—the way he tried to manipulate the situation, the way he twisted everything to suit his needs. She had been so blinded by her own ambition that she had ignored the warning signs. She had let him convince her that the company, the brand, and the perfect image were more important than anything else. But not anymore.

"Is that really all you care about?" Amanda asked, her voice rising with disbelief. "Our brand? Our image? Not me. Not us."

Tom's jaw tightened, but he didn't answer.

Amanda took a step back, feeling like the walls were closing in on her. "I'm done, Tom. I'm done living a lie."

He stood up abruptly, stepping toward her, his voice lowering with cold intent. "You don't get to just walk away from this. I'm not going to let you ruin everything we've built. You think you can just leave me? Leave us? I'll make sure you regret it."

The threat hung in the air like a dark cloud, but Amanda didn't flinch. She had heard enough. She was no longer afraid of him, of the future they had built together.

"I'll find a way out," Amanda said, her voice unwavering. "I'll dissolve the NEXT contract, and you won't be able to stop me."

Tom's eyes narrowed, his expression a mixture of frustration and fury. "You'll regret this, Amanda. You don't know what you're getting yourself into."

She turned away, her heart pounding in her chest, but for the first time in a long while, she felt a glimmer of hope. This wasn't just about ending her marriage—it was about ending her life under the control of NEXT, about breaking free from a system that had twisted everything she thought she wanted.

Later that night, she found herself in front of her phone, scrolling through contacts, until she found Trevor Kline's name.

She hesitated for a moment, knowing the risk, knowing that Tom would never forgive her for involving someone from the underground network. But she had no other choice. She needed help.

With a deep breath, Amanda sent a message to Trevor: "I need your help. I want to expose NEXT. And I need to get out before it's too late. Can you help me?"

She hit send, knowing that the response could change everything—either for the better or for the worse. Either way, she was done pretending.

CHAPTER SIXTEEN

Ben and Maria sat on their porch, the evening sun casting a golden hue over their quiet suburban home. The sky, painted with streaks of orange and pink, mirrored the calmness of their surroundings. It was the kind of scene that looked peaceful from the outside, but for them, it was more than just a picturesque view—it was a reflection of the years they'd spent building something that felt real amidst the illusion of perfection. The houses around them were neatly manicured, lawns trimmed with precision, the sidewalks straight and orderly. But as Ben and Maria looked at each other, their hands intertwined in a shared quiet understanding, they knew that their story was anything but neatly scripted. It was theirs, raw in its imperfection.

"Remember when we first met?" Maria asked, her voice soft, almost nostalgic, as though she were reaching back through the years to a time when their lives hadn't yet been entwined by fate—or algorithms.

Ben chuckled, a low, warm sound that carried the weight of memories long past. His eyes crinkled at the corners, the lines on his face deepening as he smiled. "I remember," he said, his voice tinged with humor. "You were so skeptical about the whole NEXT thing. Thought I was some kind of experiment."

Maria smiled at the memory, but there was something in her eyes—an unease, a hint of something unspoken. "I didn't trust it at first," she admitted, her voice drifting. "Still don't trust everything about it, to be honest. But you… you were different. You didn't try to sell me on some perfect fairytale. You just… were. And that made all the difference."

The simplicity of his presence, the quiet authenticity of who Ben was, had been what Maria had found most compelling. He wasn't trying to mold himself into a version of what the system said he should be. He was just him, and for her, that was everything. She could feel the weight of their shared history in that moment—their connection, forged through trials both before and after their meeting, had shaped their relationship in ways they couldn't fully grasp.

They had both come from broken marriages, their pasts shadowed by mistakes, regrets, and the kind of loss that left an imprint on your soul. Maria had once been married to a man whose ideas about love were more about control than connection. She had been suffocated by his need to possess, to dominate, to manipulate her into his idea of who she should be. By the time their marriage ended, Maria had learned to distrust the very notion of soulmates—the idea that one person could complete you, as if your identity was only half without them. Ben, on the other hand, had been a widower. His first wife's death had been sudden, unexpected. He hadn't been prepared for the void she left behind. The years that followed were spent in quiet solitude, unable to shake the feeling that he was drifting, unsure whether he would ever find someone who could fill the gap she had left, or whether he even wanted to try. And yet, when NEXT had come into their lives, promising efficiency, compatibility, and the elimination of the usual uncertainties of modern relationships, both of them had given it a shot. At first, it had seemed too good to be true—an answer to all their past disappointments.

For some, the promises of NEXT had felt hollow, manipulative even—like buying love from a vending machine. It had taken away the messiness of traditional courtship, the risks of rejection, the vulnerability of being truly seen. But for Ben and Maria, it had worked. It had matched them based on compatibility—everything from their genetic makeup to their career goals, their hobbies, their desires. At first, it had felt like fate. But now, in the stillness of the evening, with the sun fading behind the trees, it started to feel more like a puzzle that had been neatly solved.

"We just clicked," Ben said, squeezing her hand gently. The words were simple, but their weight carried something deeper—something that both of them had felt, something beyond the algorithm that had predicted they'd work well together. "No games, no pretending. It was just… easy."

Maria nodded, her face softening as she let the words settle, but there was something about them that lingered in the air between them—something unspoken. Her smile faltered for just a moment. "But is that a good thing?" she asked, her voice dropping to a more serious tone. "I mean, look at how many people are out there, stuck in a system that tells them exactly who to love and when. How do we know we wouldn't have found each other without NEXT?"

The question hung there, hanging like the heavy air before a storm. Ben looked at her, considering her words carefully. It was a question he'd thought about more times than he cared to admit. Had they truly found each other because of the algorithm, or had NEXT simply given them a push in the right direction, removing the messy, beautiful unpredictability of love?

"I don't know," Ben admitted after a long pause. His voice softened, the certainty he had once felt wavering under the weight of her question. "But the fact is, we found each other. And we're happy. That's all that matters, right?"

The simplicity of his answer was comforting, but Maria couldn't shake the feeling that something about it was too neat. Too… easy. She was silent for a while, her gaze drifting toward the horizon where the last rays of the sun were dipping below the trees. The light softened as if it too was reflecting on the weight of their conversation. She felt the pull of his words, but in the back of her mind, something began to shift. A seed of doubt had started to sprout. It wasn't that she regretted her relationship with Ben—not at all. But the more she thought about it, the more she realized how much of their love had been shaped by NEXT. The algorithm had known them before they even knew themselves, calculating everything from their likes to their dislikes, their temperaments, and their goals. It had taken away the mystery of falling in love, the thrill of discovery that comes with finding someone on your own terms. What if their connection was just the product of numbers and data? What if the true magic of love—the kind that defies reason and expectation—was something they'd never truly experienced because their bond had been created by a system that removed the uncertainty and risk? The idea felt unsettling.

"You think we could've made it without NEXT?" Ben asked, his voice softer now, tinged with an unfamiliar vulnerability. The words hung in the air between them, tentative, as though he were testing a thought that had been forming in the back of his mind for some time. His grip on her hand tightened just slightly, the weight of his question heavier than he intended.

Maria turned to face him fully, her expression shifting to one of quiet contemplation. A slight frown tugged at the corners of her lips, and she took a moment before responding, as if weighing the truth in her mind before letting it spill out. "I don't know," she admitted, her voice thoughtful but edged with uncertainty. "But I think I'd like to find out. Maybe not now. But one day. I just wonder what it would feel like if we hadn't had a system telling us we were supposed to work together. What if we had just met, like any two people who find each other by accident?"

Ben was silent for a moment, the quiet between them stretching, heavy with the weight of her words. He felt a sudden pang of unease, as if the foundation beneath their relationship, which had always felt solid and unshakable, was being questioned. Could they have made it without NEXT? The question lingered in the air like a cloud that refused to dissipate. He couldn't deny that the simplicity of their love had, in many ways, been shaped by the ease of the system—the algorithm that had decided they were a perfect match, that had guided them together without the messiness of trial and error, without the chaos of the unknown. But now, as he looked at Maria, he realized that the question was not so easily answered. She wasn't asking for something drastic; she was asking for something deeper, something more authentic than what the system had given them.

Ben opened his mouth to respond, but the words stuck in his throat. He had always been someone who valued certainty, who found comfort in knowing that the path ahead was clear. NEXT had provided that clarity. It had promised a future free from the uncertainty that had haunted his past relationships. But now, Maria was asking for something different. She wasn't rejecting their bond or the love they had built. She was simply wondering if there was more—if there was a version of their love that existed outside the confines of the algorithm, outside the system that had made it so… predictable. His mind raced as he tried to reconcile the life they had built with the doubt that had crept into Maria's thoughts. Maybe it wasn't about rejecting the system entirely, but about finding a way to reclaim something that felt more real, more organic—a relationship they had the power to shape for themselves, rather than one that had been handed to them.

Ben could feel the weight of the realization settling in his chest, heavier than he expected. "You've got a point," he said slowly, the words coming with a sense of reluctant clarity. He exhaled, a long, steady breath, as if letting go of something he hadn't even known he was holding onto. "But right now, I'm happy. And if that makes us a success story for NEXT, then maybe that's not such a bad thing. We've got each other, Maria. That's what matters."

His words, though simple, felt like an anchor in the midst of the storm Maria's doubts had stirred. But even as he spoke them, Ben knew that the truth of her question wasn't something easily dismissed. They had built their life on a foundation that wasn't entirely their own, and while that was comforting in some ways, it also left room for questions that would continue to echo long after the sun had set and the porch grew quiet again. Maria didn't respond immediately. She sat with his words, letting them settle into her mind, as if they were a puzzle piece she hadn't quite found a place for yet. She didn't want to challenge their happiness—not really. But in the depths of her thoughts, there was a longing for something more, something beyond the algorithm's calculations. She wanted to know if their connection was truly their own, or if it had been a product of a system that took away the messy beauty of falling in love on their own terms.

The evening air had grown cooler, the sun now gone, leaving only the dim glow of the porch light to illuminate their faces. In the stillness of the night, Maria could almost hear the hum of the world outside—people living their lives according to the rules of NEXT, blindly trusting the system that had shaped their fates. But as she sat next to Ben, she couldn't help but wonder if there was a different way to love—one that wasn't so neatly defined, one that didn't rely on the certainty of a match made by an algorithm. Could they, just once, take a step outside the boundaries that had been set for them? Could their love be something more than a formula?

But for now, as they sat in the quiet, with the world fading into the night around them, Maria knew one thing for sure: She wasn't alone in her doubts. Ben had heard her. And that, in itself, was a place to start.

Other Books By The Author

Tangled Hearts

Silent Vision

Silent Vision 2 Code Name Echo

Man Up

Woman Up

Couple Up

Marriage is it worth the fight

Sheltered Hearts

WYGDN what you gonna do now

Empowering the Future

Artificial Love

Beyond Loss